THE SHOOTING SCRIPT®

Little Children

Little Children

Screenplay by
Todd Field & Tom Perrotta

Based on the novel by Tom Perrotta

Introduction by
Tom Perrotta

A Newmarket Shooting Script® Series Book

NEWMARKET PRESS • NEW YORK

FIRST EDITION

10 9 8 7 6 5 4 3 2 1

ISBN: 978-1-55704-777-9

Library of Congress Catalog-in-Publication Data available upon request.

QUANTITY PURCHASES

Companies, professional groups, clubs, and other organizations may qualify for special terms when ordering quantities
of this title. For information, write to Special Sales, Newmarket Press, 18 East 48th Street, New York, NY 10017;
call (212) 832-3575 or 1-800-669-3903; FAX (212) 832-3629; or e-mail info@newmarketpress.com.

Website: www.newmarketpress.com

Manufactured in the United States of America.

OTHER BOOKS IN THE NEWMARKET SHOOTING SCRIPT® SERIES INCLUDE:

About a Boy: The Shooting Script	In Good Company: The Shooting Script
Adaptation: The Shooting Script	Little Miss Sunshine: The Shooting Script
The Age of Innocence: The Shooting Script	Man on the Moon: The Shooting Script
American Beauty: The Shooting Script	The Matrix: The Shooting Script
A Beautiful Mind: The Shooting Script	The People vs. Larry Flynt: The Shooting Script
Big Fish: The Shooting Script	Pieces of April: The Shooting Script
The Birdcage: The Shooting Script	Punch-Drunk Love: The Shooting Script
Black Hawk Down: The Shooting Script	Red Dragon: The Shooting Script
Capote: The Shooting Script	The Shawshank Redemption: The Shooting Script
Cast Away: The Shooting Script	Sideways: The Shooting Script
Cinderella Man: The Shooting Script	Snow Falling on Cedars: The Shooting Script
The Constant Gardener: The Shooting Script	The Squid and the Whale: The Shooting Script
Dead Man Walking: The Shooting Script	State and Main: The Shooting Script
Eternal Sunshine of the Spotless Mind: The Shooting Script	Stranger Than Fiction: The Shooting Script
Gods and Monsters: The Shooting Script	Traffic: The Shooting Script
Gosford Park: The Shooting Script	Thank You for Smoking: The Shooting Script
Human Nature: The Shooting Script	Transamerica: The Shooting Script
The Ice Storm: The Shooting Script	The Truman Show: The Shooting Script
	War of the Worlds: The Shooting Script

OTHER NEWMARKET PICTORIAL MOVIEBOOKS AND NEWMARKET INSIDER FILM BOOKS INCLUDE:

The Art of The Matrix*	A Good Year: Portrait of the Film
The Art of X2*	Hitchhiker's Guide to the Galaxy: The Filming of the Douglas Adams Classic
The Art of X-Men: The Last Stand	
Bram Stoker's Dracula: The Film and the Legend*	Hotel Rwanda: Bringing the True Story of an African Hero to Film*
Chicago: The Movie and Lyrics*	The Jaws Log
Dances with Wolves: The Illustrated Story of the Epic Film*	Kinsey: Public and Private*
Dreamgirls	Memoirs of a Geisha: A Portrait of the Film
E.T. The Extra-Terrestrial: From Concept to Classic*	Ray: A Tribute to the Movie, the Music, and the Man*
Gladiator: The Making of the Ridley Scott Epic Film	Saving Private Ryan: The Men, The Mission, The Movie
Good Night, and Good Luck: The Screenplay and History Behind the Landmark Movie*	Schindler's List: Images of the Steven Spielberg Film
	Tim Burton's Corpse Bride: An Invitation to the Wedding

*Includes Screenplay

CONTENTS

INTRODUCTION

TOM PERROTTA

WALKING ACROSS THE BRIDGE

"So how *was* that?" people sometimes ask me when they find out that I collaborated with writer/director Todd Field on the script for the movie based on my novel *Little Children*. They pose this question not in the spirit of objective inquiry, but with preemptive sympathy, as if I'd just informed them that I'd undergone oral surgery. Others are more forthright. "That must have been hard," they say, "giving up your baby like that."

I understand their assumption; to some degree I shared it not too long ago. It's an assumption rooted in a number of widely held beliefs that, like most truisms, turn out not always to be true—i.e., that books inevitably get mangled by the Hollywood meat grinder, that screenwriters get no respect in the movie business, and that novelists are solitary, thin-skinned neurotics ill-suited for the crass, win-some/lose-some mathematics of cinematic collaboration.

Now I'd be the last person to deny that novel writing is a solitary endeavor; that's one of the things that drew me to it in the first place. Like most writers, I enjoy silence, hate interruptions, and don't mind sitting for hours in an empty room. I used to tell myself that if the circumstances of my life had been different—if my educational and professional opportunities had been more limited than they actually were—I would've become a long-distance truck driver, because at least that way I would've been left alone.

I don't tell myself that story so much anymore, not since I quit my teaching job about six years ago and began writing full-time. After you spend more than half a decade working alone in a small, quiet room, the novelty starts to wear off a bit. You find yourself growing a little more tolerant of interruptions and diversions, maybe even eager for them. You stare long-ingly at the phone; you check your e-mail a little more than is good for you. And when the possibility arises of collaborating with Todd Field on a script based on the novel you just spent two long years committing to paper, you think, "Well, it can't hurt to meet the guy."

I can't say I knew a whole lot about Todd when Albert Berger and Ron Yerxa of Bona Fide Productions first mentioned him as a possible director for *Little Children*, but the little I did know certainly made me well-disposed to him. I knew that he'd made *In the Bedroom,* one of the most powerful American film dramas in recent memory, and that it had been based on a short story by the late Andre Dubus, a writer whose work I'd long admired. And I knew that Todd had acted in some terrific independent films in the 90s, including Nicole Holofcener's *Walking and Talking* and Victor Nunez's *Ruby in Paradise,* as well as bigger movies like *Twister* and *Eyes Wide Shut.* Plus, he loved my book. That's one sure way to get on my good side.

As a matter of fact, he loved *Little Children* so much that his first impulse was to adapt it into a multipart miniseries for HBO, so we wouldn't have to lose any of the novel's many subplots, digressions, and flashbacks. This seemed like an intriguing idea to me, but it didn't pan out. Shortly after the book was optioned by New Line Cinema, we played a brief game of *After you! No, after you!*—each one inviting the other to write the script—before finally deciding to write it together.

It's a strange thing to *write* with someone else, even a close friend, to perform a solitary, fairly intimate act with another person sitting right next to you, doing his version of the same thing; to try to do this with someone who's essentially a stranger is truly daunting. On the other hand, it's not a bad way to get to know someone. You get a good solid dose of each other all at once. Eccentricities reveal themselves quickly.

Todd, for example, talked a lot about pencils in the first few days of our collaboration. He was obsessed with Eberhard Blackwings, a hard-to-find writing utensil allegedly cherished by pencil-lovers everywhere. He showed me one, and seemed a bit disappointed by my inability to recognize its superiority to all other pencils. For his part, he grew a bit exasperated by my refusal to highlight and delete large sections of text with a single keystroke. I preferred, in my own Luddite way, to hold down the backspace key, erasing one letter at a time. I also discovered, to my dismay, that he didn't feel the need to eat on a regular schedule, which meant that I was always the one sheepishly calling for a lunch break in the middle of a crucial dramatic scene (like the playground tots in the movie, I hold on tight to my routines and timetables). If he expressed a desire to press on for a little while longer, I'd avert my eyes and mumble something about low blood sugar, shaming him into going out and getting an enormous slice of pizza at Little Steven's.

For the most part we worked in the Eliot Hotel, an elegant, old-fashioned establishment in Boston's Back Bay, located about a half hour from my home. Some days I rode my bike, but most of the time I took the bus into Harvard Square and walked down Massachusetts Avenue past M.I.T. and over the Harvard Bridge, a long, low structure that spans the Charles River, offering a breathtaking view of the city. Once I crossed the river, my route took me past an Irish pub called the Crossroads, which had been the novelist Richard Yates's home away from home when he taught at Boston University. Todd and I are both big fans of Yates, particularly his great novel, *Revolutionary Road*, which was very much on our minds as we explored our own story of frustrated young parents in the suburbs, and passing his old haunt always seemed like an auspicious way to begin the writing day.

Looking back now, I'm struck by how much of what we imagined in that hotel room ended up on the screen. Not everything, of course—there were scenes we wrote that got cut for one reason or another, scenes that got shot but didn't survive the editing process, scenes that were transformed in rehearsal, so that they seemed new and surprising to me when I saw the finished film, and scenes whose beauty and power are only hinted at on the page (I'm thinking here of both the lovely montage describing Sarah and Brad's burgeoning but still chaste relationship at the Town Pool, and the amazing sequence in which Ronnie McGorvey sets off a panic by jumping into the water on a hot day). And nothing could have prepared me for the nuances an ensemble of incredibly talented actors brought to the material—the wondrously eloquent expressions on Kate Winslet's face when she talks to her lover at the pool; the palpably close relationship between Patrick Wilson and his on-screen child (a beautiful little boy in a jester's cap); the eerie dignity Jackie Earle Haley brought to the role of Ronnie McGorvey; the almost feral quality of Phyllis Somerville's maternal love; the comic zeal Noah Emmerich brought to the loose cannon character of Larry; the force of Jennifer Connelly's epiphany when she realizes her husband's been cheating on her; I could go on and on. But even taking all this into account, it was clear to me when I saw the movie that the heart of our script had somehow survived the journey onto the screen.

For me, at least, the single most distinctive feature of both the script and the film is the Voice, the calm, paternal narrator whose sober commentary provides such a welcome contrast to the overwrought actions of the characters. Todd described this Voice to me in our very first meeting, explaining that he wanted *Frontline*'s Will Lyman to play the part. Throughout the entire writing process, Todd imitated the Voice with such uncanny accuracy that, by the time I saw the finished film, I couldn't help feeling that Will Lyman was impersonating Todd Field, and not vice versa. I had a similar feeling of déjà vu when I saw the footage of the climactic football game, which was done as a sort of parody/homage to those highlight reels put together by NFL Films, and which Todd had also described to me in detail before we began the script.

But if the core of the movie survived intact from our earliest conversations, other parts evolved more gradually. The ending of the movie—the scenes that diverge most clearly from the novel—emerged through a classic process of trial and error. Todd and I wrote a draft of the script that hewed closely to the ending in the book, but we were both dissatisfied, along with our producers. It was clear that while a quiet, contemplative ending might work in a 350-page novel, a two-hour movie packed full of tension required something a little more dramatic. We kicked around some ideas, but didn't make a whole lot of headway. When Todd finally called me on a Saturday morning and described the extreme act that now completes the arc of the film, I thought at first that he was kidding me. It seemed like too big a leap to me—too melodramatic, too intense, nothing I would do on my own. But the more I thought about it, the clearer it became that the act in question not only made sense within the context of the film—it seemed, in a strange way, almost inevitable. And now, when I see it up on the screen, it's hard for me to imagine it any other way.

"So how *was* that?"

This is how it was.

Every once in a while, these days, I find myself walking across the Harvard Bridge into the city. And every time I do this, a funny feeling comes over me, maybe halfway across the span. For just a second or two I lose track of the present moment, and it seems to me that I'm heading toward the Crossroads and the ghost of Richard Yates on my way to the Eliot Hotel, and when I get there Todd will be standing on the corner, taking the last guilty drag on a cigarette he knows he shouldn't be smoking, and there's a full day's work ahead of us. It's a happy, optimistic feeling, and I remember it well from the days when we wrote this script.

—November 2006

<u>Little Children</u>

Screenplay
by
Todd Field & Tom Perrotta

Based on the novel
by
Tom Perrotta

25 July 2005

FADE IN:

SIGHTS & SOUNDS OF WINDING MOVEMENTS ON VARIOUS TIMEPIECES.

Tick Tock, the rhythm overwhelming: Ansonia shelf, wall, mantel, long-case, table, and bracket. Each movement open escapement.

THE HARD SCREAMING OF A RAIL ENGINE

HOUSE AFTER HOUSE — TOWN AFTER TOWN — AS SEEN FROM A TRAIN.

The strains of a NEWSCAST.

An ANCHOR WOMAN front and center, super-imposed images behind her.

> ANCHOR WOMAN
> It has only been two weeks since an East
> Wyndam man, Ronald James McGorvey
> returned home from prison after serving
> a two-year sentence for indecent
> exposure to a minor. And already a
> grassroots movement is clamoring to
> remove him from the community.

News B-Roll: BADLY XEROXED FLYERS on TELEPHONE POLES depicting a plump man with wiry, thinning hair and an anxious expression. In bold script it reads: *Are your children safe?*

> ANCHOR WOMAN
> The group is called *The Committee of
> Concerned Parents.*

A CLOSER DETAIL on the BOTTOM EDGE identifies the supplier of the flyer as *The Committee of Concerned Parents.*

> ANCHOR WOMAN
> Police are advising parents to...

The newscast continues as we WIDEN within a dark livingroom to REVEAL A MAN sitting in a LA-Z-BOY watching the broadcast. His hand grips a glass of soda and ice. He takes a sip.

BLACK. COMPLETE SILENCE. A LEGEND APPEARS: LITTLE CHILDREN

Then —

> WOMAN'S VOICE
> My husband and I had an actual spiritual
> experience...

EXT. WALKER STREET PLAYGROUND — DAY

This is THERESA, mid-thirties, a pale woman, but in her time a real beauty.

> THERESA
> ...we were on our vacation in Cabo with
> eight other couples, and this Mayan
> woman... a goddess, just a goddess...

CUT TO:

MARY ANN, mid-thirties, toothpick-thin, uptight, and clad in
CATALOGUE CASUAL.

                    MARY ANN
      She's due in September. She says she's
      gonna take three months off, and be back
      to work before Christmas. *Please.* Six
      months from now she'll be right here on
      this bench with us...

                                  CUT TO:

CHERYL, a woman who has the unfortunate habit of ending her sentences
with an upwardy teenagery question mark.

                    CHERYL
      Well, my friend Beth said the way she did
      it, was to just take him with her every
      time she went to the bathroom.

                    MARY ANN
      I find that strange.

                    CHERYL
      That's what I said to Beth.

                    MARY ANN
      It's oedipal.

                    THERESA
      What's the rush? Although, I will say
      when I was potty training Christian? I
      opened the diaper and it was huge, like a
      grown man.

Snatches of the women talking begin a slow diminuendo, as they shift
to the subject of pre-schools.

On the bench opposite the women is SARAH PIERCE, 30. It is through
Sarah's ears that we have been introduced to these ladies. And because
of this, our idea of them may be less than kind.

As we PUSH IN on her — A NEW VOICE EMERGES. IT IS MALE, CALM, AND NON-
JUDGMENTAL, IN SHORT, GROWN-UP.

                    VOICE
      Smiling politely to mask a familiar
      feeling of desperation, Sarah reminded
      herself to think like an anthropologist.
      She was a researcher studying the
      behavior of typical suburban women. She
      was *not* a typical suburban woman herself.

                    CHERYL
      John and I were having sex the other
      night, and I drifted off right in the
      middle of it.

                    THERESA
        (chuckles sympathetically)
      It happens.

                         CHERYL
          I guess. But when I woke up and
          apologized? He said he hadn't even
          noticed.

                         MARY ANN
          You know what you should do? Set aside a
          specific block of time for making love.
          That's what Lewis and I do. Every Tuesday
          night at nine o'clock.

                         VOICE
          Whether you want to or not, Sarah
          thought, her eyes straying over to the
          play area...

CHRISTIAN, Theresa's son, pummels Mary Ann's cowering TROY and —

Cheryl's COURTNEY shows Mary Ann's ISABELLE her *DORA THE EXPLORER*
underpants.

                         VOICE
          Even at such a tiny playground as this,
          Lucy didn't interact much with the other
          children.

Sarah's three-year-old daughter, LUCY, stands alone near the top of
the slide. She appears to be talking to herself.

Sarah takes her in.

                         VOICE
          Sarah didn't really know why they even
          bothered coming here, except that she'd
          probably go crazy, trapped in the house
          all day with this unknowable little
          person.

CLOSE ON a watch face. The second hand sweeps past twelve...

                         VOICE
          Morning snack time was ten thirty on the
          dot. A regimen established and maintained
          by Mary Ann...

MARY ANN's face fills the screen as she turns and soundlessly barks
toward the playground.

                         VOICE
          ...who believed that rigid adherence to a
          timetable...

The children all turn toward Mary Ann in SLOW MOTION and start
running in her direction.

                         VOICE
          ...was not only the key to a healthy
          marriage, but to effective parenting as
          well.

CLOSE ON HANDS DIGGING THROUGH A DIAPER BAG.

> LUCY (O.C.)
> Mommy?

All the kids, and their mothers are gathered around a picnic table, shoveling CHEERIOS and GOLDFISH into their mouths —

Except for Sarah who is crouched down on the grass a few feet away rummaging through a diaper bag. Lucy stands facing her mother, an anxious look on the child's face.

> LUCY
> Where my snack?

> SARAH
> (digging through bag)
> I'm sure it's in here somewhere.

> LUCY
> Where it went? Where my snack?

> SARAH
> I'm sorry, honey. Mommy can't find it.
> (to other mothers)
> I forgot the rice cakes. I must have left them on the counter.

AT THE PICNIC BENCH the three women, and their offspring watch the drama that is playing out on the grass before them.

> CHERYL
> Poor thing.

> LUCY (O.C.)
> I want my snaaaack!

> MARY ANN
> (pointed)
> That's the second time this week.

> THERESA
> It's hard to keep track of everything.

> LUCY (O.C.)
> Bad Mommy, bad mommy, bad mommy.

BACK TO SARAH & LUCY

> SARAH
> (pleading)
> Just calm down.

> LUCY
> No! No calm down!

> SARAH
> It's not here.

Sarah hands her the bag.

                              SARAH
                    Alright, here. See for yourself.

Lucy looks into the bag, and then throws it at her mother's head.
Sarah winds up with the strap dangling around her neck.

                              MARY ANN
                    <u>Wait</u>!

This single word radiates with such undeniable adult authority that
everything stops.

                              MARY ANN
                    Troy, honey? Give Lucy your Goldfish.

                              TROY
                    No!

He turns his body, forming a barrier between Lucy and his snack.

                              MARY ANN
                    Troy Jonathan. Give me those Goldfish.

                              TROY
                         (whimpering)
                    But mama, they're mine.

                              MARY ANN
                    No backtalk. You can share with your
                    sister.

With no further word of protest, Troy hands the BAG to Mary Ann.

                              SARAH
                         (to Lucy)
                    Go and sit down. Troy has goldfish for
                    you.

Lucy runs over to join the others at the picnic bench.

                              SARAH
                         (to Mary Ann)
                    Thank you. You're a lifesaver.

                              MARY ANN
                    It's nothing. I just hate to see her
                    suffer like that.

Sarah gets down on one knee and begins refilling the diaper bag.

                              MARY ANN
                    Maybe you should make a check list, tape
                    it to the door so it's the last thing you
                    see before leaving the house. That's what
                    I do.

Sarah looks up, forcing a smile.

                              SARAH
                    Thank you. That's a really helpful
                    suggestion.

Cheryl's head darts away from the other mothers. She reaches across the table and grabs Theresa's hand.

                    CHERYL
               (soft and urgent)
          Look.

Theresa glances instinctively toward the PLAY STRUCTURE.

                    THERESA
          What?

                    CHERYL
          Over there. The Prom King?

                    THERESA
               (smiling)
          Oh my God. He's back.

Sarah looks up from the diaper bag.

                    VOICE
          Sarah followed the other women's gazes
          over to the entrance of the playground,
          eager to finally get a glimpse of the
          Prom King...

In the middle distance, we see a strapping BLOND MAN enter through the park's iron gate. He pushes a DOUBLE STROLLER. One side is empty and the other is occupied by a large STUFFED BEAR. The man's three-year-old son sits perched on his father's shoulders. He wears a JESTER'S CAP, and shoots his arms out as if he is flying.

                    VOICE
          ... the handsome and mysterious young
          father who had been a regular at the
          Walker Street Playground for several
          weeks this past spring, before abruptly
          dropping out of sight.

With the ease of someone performing a familiar action, the man lifts his son off his shoulders, and gallops around the play structure. The boy squeals as the man bobs, hops, and weaves - giving the boy the time of his life. Unlike the young mothers on the benches watching their children from a distance, this man is engaged. As if he couldn't imagine doing anything else, with anyone else. More playmate than parent.

                    VOICE
          His departure had left a gaping hole in
          the emotional lives of Cheryl, Theresa,
          and Mary Ann. Barely a day went by
          without one of them speculating wistfully
          about the reason for his absence and the
          likelihood of his return.

                    BRAD (O.C.)
          ... ninety eight ... ninety nine ...

INT. BRAD'S HOUSE, LIVING ROOM — DAY

The blond man from the playground rises in and out of frame. This is BRAD ADAMSON, 30. He is sweating, and breathing heavily, at the end of a long circuit of daily push-ups.

> BRAD
> ... One hundred.

KITCHEN

Brad, wearing PLAY-TEX GLOVES, stands at the sink doing dishes.

HALLWAY

Brad vacuums.

LIVING ROOM — LATER (MAGIC)

Brad and Aaron sit on the floor engrossed in their favorite activity: Train Wreck, a brutally simple game. GORDON and PERCY, two characters from *Thomas the Tank Engine,* move in opposite directions around a circular track, making happy CHUGGING SOUNDS right up to the moment of an inevitable collision.

> AARON
> (shouting)
> Splang!

This is the sound effect that always accompanies the crash.

> AARON
> Take that, Gordon.

> BRAD
> Ouch! That hurt, Percy.

Aaron laughs uproariously at Brad's pain.

> AARON
> Again! Again!

They set-up for another go, and repeat the game.

The game ends abruptly though, as Aaron scrambles to his feet and stares toward the The SOUND of someone coming through the FRONT DOOR.

> AARON
> Mommy!

He rips the Jester cap off his head and flings it away.

Brad watches the haberdashery make a wide arc in the air. He cannot take his eyes from it. Time seems to momentarily stop.

> VOICE
> The Jester's cap was something that truly disturbed Brad. All day long The boy ate, played, and napped in it. He would burst into tears if his Father had so much suggested it be removed.

                              VOICE (CONT)
                    But the moment his Mother stepped in the
                    house he had no more use for it, as if the
                    entire day up to that point had been a
                    pointless and somewhat useless charade.

Aaron flies into the arms of KATHY, 30, and lovely. She drops to one
knee, and holds her arms out wide.

                              KATHY
                    I missed you so so so so much.

He buries his face against her chest; she strokes his head.

                              KATHY
                    You got some color, didn't you? Did daddy
                    forget the sunscreen again?

Brad stares down at the engine he still holds. Gordon's peevish
expression feels like it's mocking him.

INT. BRAD'S HOUSE, KITCHEN — MAGIC

Brad, Kathy & Aaron sit around the table at the tail end of dinner.

                              BRAD
                    I think I'm gonna finally break down and
                    get a mobile phone.

                              KATHY
                    Really? Why?

                              BRAD
                    I have no way of reaching you when I'm
                    out with Aaron.

                              KATHY
                         (to Aaron)
                    You're done, right?

She rises to clear the boy's dish, and carries it over to the sink.

                              BRAD
                    ...you've got one. Don't you think it's
                    strange I don't?

                              KATHY
                    Yeah, I do. You just never wanted one
                    before.

She wets a towel, and heads back over to Aaron.

                              BRAD
                    Yeah, I know. There's a family plan. We
                    can talk for free.

Kathy cleans the dinner from Aaron's face, and in the process turns
her back on an uncomfortable fiscal conversation.

                              KATHY
                    Let's see where we are at the end of the
                    month.

EXT. MAIN STREET — TWILIGHT

Carrying a briefcase, Brad walks alone along an empty street. He passes an SUV swathed in graphics for the *National Guard:* A recruiting vehicle, and handy piece of mobile advertisement. A TRIO OF DRAB GREEN CLAD SOLDIERS stare back at him: defiant and brave.

> VOICE
> As was her custom, each weeknight after dinner, the boy's mother sent Brad down to the Municipal library to study for the bar exam...

EXT. MUNICIPAL LIBRARY — TWILIGHT

> VOICE
> ...but he never quite made it through the door of the building.

Brad settles in on a bench. About twenty yards away, FOUR SKATEBOARDERS, ages thirteen to sixteen, dressed in knee-length shorts, baggy T-shirts, and fashionably retro sneakers - jump stairs, metal railings, and retaining walls around a square granite building. They are all armed with iPODS & MOBILE PHONES.

> VOICE
> Brad had been watching the boys for weeks now, sometimes for as long as an hour at a stretch, but he'd never received the slightest acknowledgement from any of them.

Brad stares longingly.

> VOICE
> He had been the same age as these boys when his mother died.

ONE OF THE BOYS, the one the others call *G*, ramps off a wall and sails into the air. He possesses an almost mystical connection to his board. *G* returns to the group, who congratulate him on his last ride.

> VOICE
> *I must have been like this*, Brad sometimes thought. *I must have been one of them.*

> MARY ANN (O.C.)
> He should just be castrated.

EXT. WALKER STREET PLAYGROUND — DAY

CLOSE ON the same handbill from the news broadcast, with the addition of a stepped-up headline: *Decent people Beware!!! There is a Pervert Among US!*

The MOTHERS all stare down at the FLYER on the picnic table.

> MARY ANN
> Quick and clean. Just chop it off. Then you wouldn't have to worry about notifying the neighbors.

                    SARAH
          You know what else you should do? Nail
          his penis above the entrance to the
          elementary school. You know, as a warning
          to other perverts.

Cheryl and Theresa chuckle politely at her sarcasm. Mary Ann is not
amused, and fixes Sarah with an icy glare.

                    MARY ANN
          You think this is funny?

                    SARAH
          I just can't believe you want to castrate
          a man for indecent exposure.

                    THERESA
          My brother used to expose himself, when
          we were teenagers. He'd do it in my
          bedroom, or in the backseat of the car,
          even at the dinner table. He always
          figured out a way to do it so that no one
          could see what he was up to but me.

                    MARY ANN
                (disgusted)
          Didn't you tell anyone?

                    THERESA
                (puzzled)
          No. I didn't want to get him in trouble.
          It didn't stop until he went away to
          college.

                    SARAH
          He should have been castrated.

                    MARY ANN
                (snapping)
          It's not the same thing. He wasn't doing
          it to strangers.

Cheryl's head swivels as if pulled by a magnet.

                    CHERYL
          Oh My God, look! After all this time.
          There he is. Two days in a row?

Brad and Aaron have arrived at the playground gate.

                    SARAH
          Maybe he just needed a vacation.

                    MARY ANN
                (suspicious)
          From what?

                    THERESA
          From being the Prom King.

                              CHERYL
                    It's a dirty job.
                              (chuckling)
                    But someone's got to do it.

As Brad and Aaron pass the women on their way over to the far swing-
set, the trio go completely silent — pretending not to notice.

Sarah watches them — amused.

                              SARAH
                    What's he do for a living?

The others look nervous, and ignore the question.

                              MARY ANN
                              (uncomfortable)
                    We've never actually spoken to him.

                              SARAH
                    You're kidding right?

                              THERESA
                    We don't even know his name.

                              SARAH
                    Really? I thought you said he was a
                    regular here.

                              THERESA
                    It was awkward.

                              CHERYL
                    He made us nervous. You had to think
                    about what you were going to wear in the
                    morning? Put on makeup? It was
                    exhausting?

Lucy leaves her position at the top of the SLIDE and wanders over to
the SWING-SET right next to where Brad pushes Aaron. She calls to her
mother.

                              LUCY
                    Mommy! Push me!

                              SARAH
                    Alright. I'll be right there.

Sarah smiles at the women, wondering how they'll react to her impending
proximity to "The Prom King." As she rises to go, Theresa calls out.

                              THERESA (O.C.)
                    Wait!

Sarah stops.

                              SARAH
                    What?

Theresa holds up her WALLET, smirking like a schoolgirl.

THERESA
Five bucks if you get his phone number.

SWING SET — MOMENTS LATER

Aaron observes Lucy with a certain amount of skepticism as she swings in near-unison beside him. He turns to Sarah, his expression unexpectedly serious.

AARON
How old is she?

SARAH
(coaxing)
Lucy, honey. Tell the nice boy how old you are.

AARON
I'm three!

He jabs the corresponding fingers into the air.

AARON
My grandmother lives in New Jersey! She doesn't have a swim pool.

SARAH
(to the boy)
Do you like to swim?

AARON
I don't like sharks. They eat you up.

BRAD
Don't listen to him. We go to the town pool almost every day.

Brad smiles at Sarah.

BRAD
I'm Brad, by the way.

She smiles back.

SARAH
Sarah.

BRAD
You guys come here a lot?

SARAH
Only for the last few weeks. We used to go to the one over on Harris, with the big wood things, and the slide across.

BRAD
Yeah, we actually rent a place right around the corner from there on Ashforth. But that ice cream truck never leaves — what a nightmare.

> SARAH
> Tell me about it.

> BRAD
> ...you know, you're the first person here
> who's ever talked to me.

> SARAH
> You make them nervous.

> BRAD
> Oh, right. I guess they don't see too
> many fathers here during the weekdays.

They keep pushing the children.

> BRAD
> You don't have to be polite. Go ahead and ask.

> SARAH
> What?

> BRAD
> What the person who wears the pants in
> the family does for a living.

> SARAH
> Alright, what does your wife do?

> BRAD
> She makes documentaries.

> SARAH
> Oh, wow. Like, *Michael Moore?*

> BRAD
> Like, PBS.

> SARAH
> Oh... well, I think it's admirable that
> you're here. There's no reason men can't
> be primary caregivers.

> BRAD
> I finished law school two years ago. But
> I can't seem to pass the bar exam. Failed
> it twice now.

> SARAH
> Maybe you just don't want to be a lawyer.

Brad looks momentarily startled by this suggestion.

> BRAD
> I'll take the test one more time. If I
> mess up now, I'm just going to have to
> find something else to do with my life.

They go back to their swinging.

                              VOICE
          Sarah was shocked by how Brad delivered
          this confession, with no apparent sense
          of being in the least bit embarrassed by
          his failure. Most men weren't like this.
          Her husband, Richard, certainly wasn't.
          She wondered if Brad was always this
          forthcoming. If anything, he seemed a
          little lonely, all too ready to open his
          heart at the slightest sign of interest,
          like a lot of young mothers she knew.

Sarah breaks the silence.

                              SARAH
          I couldn't help noticing your stroller.
          Do you have another child?

                              BRAD
          Just Aaron. We got that at a yard sale.
          The extra seat comes in handy for the
          bear.

                              SARAH
          Lucy refuses to be put into a stroller,
          or a car seat. We have to walk everywhere.
          It takes us half an hour to go three
          blocks, unless I carry her.

                              AARON
          Daddy finish.

                              BRAD
          You sure? We just got here.

                              ARRON
          Daaady, I finish right now.

                              BRAD
          Alright. One, two, three.

He stops the swing, leaves Aaron, and attends to the bear. He pulls
it out of the swing, and straps it into the stroller. Then comes back
for Aaron.

Sarah watches in silence as he cups Aaron by the armpits and attempts
to lift him out of the swing.

The boy's foot gets caught in one of the apertures, and she hurries
over to free it before Brad has a chance to ask for assistance.

                              BRAD
          Thanks.

                              SARAH
          No problem.

Sarah watches as Brad buckles Aaron into the stroller.

                         VOICE
          It was then, while watching Brad kneel
          down at his son's feet, that Sarah found
          herself gripped by an unexpected pang of
          sadness.

She looks toward the opposite end of the playground — The women
leaning forward on their bench, completely riveted.

                         VOICE
          Don't go, she thought. *Don't leave me
          here with the others.*

Brad stands and turns toward her, as if he'd read her mind.

                         BRAD
                    (curious smile)
          Well, it was nice talking to you.

                         SARAH
          Yeah, you too.

He starts to leave.

                         SARAH
                    (suddenly)
          Hey.

Brad stops and looks at her, confused.

                         BRAD
          Yes?

                         SARAH
                    (conspiratorial)
          Come here.

                         BRAD
          What?

                         SARAH
          Just...come here.

He does as he's told.

                         SARAH
          You see those women over there?

He glances in the direction of the PICNIC TABLE. All of the women
suddenly look in the other direction

                         SARAH
          Yeah. Don't look. Don't look. You know
          what they call you?

He takes a small step toward Sarah, intrigued.

                         BRAD
          What?

                         SARAH
          The Prom King.

                         BRAD
          Ouch. That's awful.

                         SARAH
          They mean it as a compliment. You're a
          big character in their fantasy lives.

                         BRAD
          Wow.

                         SARAH
          One of them bet me five dollars I
          couldn't get your phone number.

                         BRAD
                    (smiling)
          Five bucks, huh?

                         SARAH
          Yep.

Brad shoots another look at the women.

                         BRAD
                    (teasing)
          Could we split it fifty-fifty?

                         SARAH
                    (right back at him)
          It could be arranged.

A moment.

                         SARAH
          Doesn't have to be your real number.

                         BRAD
          Well, in that case, sure.

Brad pats himself down, looking for a pen. Nothing.

                         BRAD
          You got a pen?

Sarah doesn't. She glances toward the table where her diaper bag is.
She doesn't want to go there. She looks back to him.

                         SARAH
          Oh, shit. No, no I don't.

                         BRAD
          Well, maybe next time.

He turns to go, but Sarah reaches out and grabs his arm.

                         SARAH
          No, listen wait...just wait.

He's waiting. She's thinking. Then —

              SARAH
      You know what would really be funny?

              BRAD
      What?

              SARAH
      ...if you gave me a hug.

              BRAD
        (smiles)
      You think?

              SARAH
      ...yeah.

Brad grins. He's game.

              BRAD
      Well, alright come here.

Brad opens his arms, and Sarah steps into them. They hug.

              MARY ANN (O.C.)
      Oh, My God!

Mary Ann's reaction makes them both start to giggle.

              SARAH
        (whispers)
      You wanna really freak them out?

Brad looks at her a moment. Then —

              BRAD
      ...Yeah.

He leans down and gives her a tentative kiss, half-serious, as if they're acting in a play.

A COLLECTIVE GASP travels from the ladies at the picnic table to our couple. Followed by a panicky chorus call from the mothers, summoning their children from the play structure.

Brad & Sarah part... But they somehow can't take their eyes off each other.

              SARAH
        (glancing at the exodus)
      I think that worked.

Both of them are blushing.

              BRAD
        (per panicky mothers)
      ...yeah, I think so.

              BRAD
      Well, it was nice meeting you.

                         SARAH
              ...yep, mmm hmmm.

He sets off without another word. Sarah watches his broad back recede
as he pushes the stroller past the other mothers, and out of the park
gates.

She turns to Lucy, sitting motionless in the swing, watching the same
sight as her mother, her feet kicking dreamily in the air.

                         SARAH
              Let's go.

She gathers Lucy from the swing, and carries her like a piece of
oversized luggage back to the bench to retrieve her things. Her face
burning with pride and with shame.

Cheryl and Theresa huddle with their children, staring at Sarah in
complete bewilderment. Flanked by Troy and Isabelle, Mary Ann looks
furious.

                         MARY ANN
              I'm sure your daughter found that very
              educational.

Sarah reaches down for the diaper bag, and turns to go.

                         SARAH
              His name's Brad. He's a lawyer. And he's
              really very nice.

Sarah picks up Lucy and heads home.

EXT. FIELD — DAY

Sarah sits under a tree trying her level best to read Margaret
Atwood's *The Handmaid's Tale.* After a moment, she puts it down, and
gazes off, distracted.

                         VOICE
              For the past few days, Sarah hadn't
              been able to concentrate on anything
              but the Prom King...and the curious
              thing that had happened between them
              on the playground.

She glances the other direction, where, some distance away —

LUCY squats on the grass, her back to Sarah, playing alone, and
talking to herself.

Sarah looks away from the child, and away into the expanse.

                         VOICE
              She didn't feel shame or guilt, only a
              sense of profound disorientation, as if
              she had been kidnapped by aliens, and
              then released, unharmed, a few hours
              later.

Mother and child under the shade of the tree. In the distance, an
amphitheater of sorts, a white wing which resembles a flying saucer.

EXT. MUNICIPAL LIBRARY — NIGHT

G the skateboarder does a series of spectacular jumps. The SOUND of wheels on concrete is deafening. A slow diminuendo into —

> VOICE
> As he had so often in recent days...

BRAD sits on his usual bench under the beech tree. But instead of watching the skateboarders, he closes his eyes. We PUSH IN ON his dreamy face.

> VOICE
> ...Brad mentally re-enacted the kiss by
> the swingset. He still couldn't believe
> it had really happened, and with all
> those women and children watching.

WE SEE AARON in his stroller at the playground that day looking up toward Brad and Sarah.

> VOICE
> Aaron had been particularly curious about
> what he'd seen.

IN BRAD'S LIVING ROOM he situates a BLOW-UP PUNCHING CLOWN. Aaron stands opposite his father.

> AARON
> Why you hugging that lady?

> BRAD
> Well, see now, that's what I'm trying to
> show you here with Bozo.

Brad kneels down in front of the clown.

> BRAD
> Sometimes it's a game grown-ups play when
> their friends.

He spreads his arms in an exaggerated way.

> BRAD
> See?

Brad mechanically embraces the clown.

> BRAD
> Hi, I'm your friend.

The boy's face wears a dubious look.

> VOICE
> Aaron was skeptical.

> VOICE
> They returned to the playground the
> following morning...

BRAD and AARON arrive to an empty PLAYGROUND.

                         VOICE
          ...but no one was there.

BRAD AND AARON at the TOWN POOL. Brad scans the other FACES.

                         VOICE
          Sarah hadn't shown up at the town pool,
          either, though Brad remembered telling
          her that he and Aaron could be found
          there most afternoons. It didn't seem to
          matter that Sarah wasn't his type...
          ...wasn't even that pretty, at least not
          compared to Kathy...

IDEALIZED VISIONS of KATHY, in the way the voice describes.

                         VOICE
          ...who had long legs, and lustrous hair,
          and perfect breasts.

BRAD continues his daydreaming.

                         VOICE
          Sarah was short, and boyish — and had
          eyebrows that were thicker than Brad
          thought necessary.

All that is described above is seen.

                         VOICE
          But even so, she'd walked into his arms
          that day, as if she was fulfilling a
          secret wish he hadn't remembered making.

                         MAN (O.C.)
          Hey, pervert!

Brad's eyes open, startled awake from his fantasy.

                         MAN (O.C.)
          Yeah you, pervert!

Brad cringes, as he looks toward —

A VAN parked by the curb directly across from him. A man gestures
toward Brad from the vehicle's dark cab.

                         MAN
          Like little boys, do you?

The teasing note in the Man's voice is clearer now, and Brad drops his
guard and squints into the van.

Meet LARRY HEDGES, 30. He wears a T-SHIRT with the word *GUARDIANS*
across the chest, and GRAY ATHLETIC SHORTS. He leans across the
passenger seat into the street-light, and grins at Brad.

                         BRAD
          Larry?

                    LARRY
          Yeah, it's fucking Larry.

                    BRAD
          Jesus, don't even joke about that.

                    LARRY
          What are you doing right now? You busy?

                    BRAD
          Uh, actually, I'm supposed to be
          studying.

Brad lifts his briefcase.

                    BRAD
          I'm taking the bar exam next month.

                    LARRY
          Didn't you do that last year?

                    BRAD
          Yeah. See how well I did?

Larry laughs. He pops the lock on the passenger side.

                    LARRY
          Get in. I got a better idea.

Brad hesitates.

                    LARRY
          C'mon, c'mon, c'mon.

Brad does as he is told.

INT/EXT. LARRY'S VAN — NIGHT

As Brad climbs in, Larry clears off the passenger seat. He tosses a
FOOTBALL and a pair of BINOCULARS into the back, and lifts up a fat
stack of BLUE PAPER.

                    LARRY
          You mind?

He drops the stack onto Brad's lap.

                    LARRY
          I'm trying to keep them nice.

Brad glances at the top sheet. It's the same flyer we've seen
throughout the story. His eyes stray to the bottom of the page:
PAID FOR BY THE COMMITTEE OF CONCERNED PARENTS.

                    BRAD
          You part of the committee?

                    LARRY
          I *am* the committee.

                    BRAD
          Wow, that's quite a commitment.

                    LARRY
                (proud)
          Yeah.

                    BRAD
          Aren't you full time on the force
          already?

Larry puts the van into gear, and pulls into the street.

                    LARRY
                (uncomfortable)
          ...I'm taking a little time off.

INT. LARRY'S VAN, MOVING — SAME

                    BRAD
                (somewhat impressed)
          How'd you find out about this creep?

                    LARRY
          There's a web site. The state's required
          to disclose the whereabouts of convicted
          sex offenders. Don't you check it?

                    BRAD
                (covering)
          Not on a regular basis.

Larry's expression darkens.

                    LARRY
          They should just castrate the bastard and
          be done with it.

Brad nods as noncommittally as he can.

A moment. In the silence, a familiar tune plays softly on the van's
stereo system.

                    BRAD
          You a Raffi fan?

                    LARRY
                (startled)
          What?

                    BRAD
          That's Raffi, right? *Big, Beautiful
          Planet*?

                    LARRY
          Ah, shit.

Larry punches the eject.

                    LARRY
          After a while I don't even know what I'm
          listening to anymore.

Larry stares at Brad, a lingering appraisal.

Brad tries to ignore how uncomfortable this feels.

                    LARRY
          You look good. Been going to the gym?

                    BRAD
          Push-ups, crunches. A little running.

                    LARRY
              (to himself)
          The guys are gonna love this.

                    BRAD
              (a bit anxious)
          What guys?

EXT. EAST WYNDAM BOMBERS' FIELD — NIGHT

Brad and Larry head across a running track, passing A SURLY-LOOKING
GUY IN A WHEELCHAIR. This is BULLHORN BOB, a fixture at the stadium.

Brad pauses at the edge of the field, a taut blue-green skin of
ARTIFICIAL TURF glowing with Caribbean purity beneath dazzling
lights. Crisp WHITE LINES and NUMBERS run from one end zone to the
other. Between the forty yard lines, a half-dozen men toss FOOTBALLS
to each other, and do warm-ups.

                    BRAD
          Wow. This is something.

                    LARRY
          It's pretty. But it doesn't have a lot
          of give. Like playing on cement.

They approach midfield. Some players strut up to greet them - TOMMY
CORRENTI, a drill-sergeant of a man, with an off-kilter nose, and A
COMICALLY NASAL VOICE, DEWAYNE ROGERS, a squat, bald African-
American man, BART WILLIAMS, a no-neck white guy with thinning hair
wearing a KNEE BRACE, RICHIE MURPHY, a powerful man with red hair,
and PETE OLAFFSON, a scrawny man whose uniform is intentionally one
size too small.

Larry steps away from Brad and button-holes DeWayne, corralling him
away from the others.

                    LARRY
          Hey, DeWayne, I really need to talk to
          you about the committee. It'd mean a lot
          to have your support on this thing.

                    DEWAYNE
          I told you already Larry. None of us are
          gonna get involved with that shit — we're
          here to play ball. If that's your thing,
          fine. But leave us out of it man. We
          can't —

                           LARRY
                   (cutting him off, pissed)
               I get it, I get it.

Larry makes a piercing whistle. The guys all turn toward him.

                           LARRY
               Bring it in. C'mon, hustle it up.

The men all gather around Larry.

                           LARRY
               Guys. I want you all to meet our new
               quarterback.

Looking slightly out of place in his cargo shorts and polo shirt,
Brad stares at Larry in bewilderment.

                           BRAD
               Quarterback?

                           CORRENTI
               He better not be a pussy.

                           LARRY
               He played in college.

                           BRAD
               I'm a little behind the curve. Who are
               you guys?

                           LARRY
               We're *The Guardians*.

                           DEWAYNE
               We're cops.

                           PETE
               Welcome to the Tri-County Touch Football
               Night League.

                           BART
               Our old quarterback's wife made him quit.
               Too many concussions.

Brad's glance strays to Bullhorn Bob, who stares back from his
wheelchair.

                           BRAD
               I thought you said it was touch.

The Guardians laugh knowingly.

                           CORRENTI
               It's tackle. We just call it touch for
               insurance purposes.

                           LARRY
               Why don't we work on some simple pass
               patterns?

Brad hesitates.

> VOICE
> Brad waited for his good sense to kick
> in. There were lots of excuses available
> to him.

He takes in his surroundings, and the faces of the other men.

> VOICE
> But it felt so good to be standing here
> beneath the bright lights. And he was
> filled with a feeling similar to the one
> he'd had right before kissing Sarah, like
> his world had cracked open to reveal a
> thrilling new possibility.

His face fills with certainty.

> BRAD
> Alright. Just let me warm up a little.

CUT TO: IMAGE OF BRAD TAKING THE SNAP AT PRACTICE.

He drops back to pass, and zips a bullet to DeWayne, totally
oblivious as Correnti enters from his blind side and smashes him to
the turf with a VICIOUS CHEAP SHOT. Brad bounces up, angry and
confused, to confront his attacker.

> BRAD
> What the fuck? That was a late hit.

> CORRENTI
> This isn't Pop Warner, Ace.

BULLHORN BOB TAUNTS BRAD FROM THE SIDELINES.

> BULLHORN BOB
> (amplified)
> You fucking faggot. You call yourself a
> quarterback?

EXT. MCGORVEY HOUSE — NIGHT

Larry's van pulls up in front of a well-tended Cape.

> BRAD
> This isn't me. You turned too soon. I'm
> on Ashforth.

Larry doesn't answer. He just stares out the window at the house.

> BRAD
> What're we doing here?

Larry presses on his horn three times, Brad startles to attention.

> BRAD
> Why'd you do that?

                    LARRY
         I want this scumbag to know I'm keeping
         an eye on him.

They sit for a long moment. It suddenly dawns on Brad whose house
this is.

                    BRAD
         Oh, God...I don't think we wanna be here,
         Larry.

                    LARRY
         It's not a question of *want*.

Larry reaches into the back seat for his BINOCULARS and trains them
on the house.

                    LARRY
         Joanie thinks I'm obsessed with this
         creep. She thinks if I had a job I
         wouldn't be driving past his house five,
         six times a day. But you know what? I
         kinda feel like this *is* my job.

Larry puts down the binoculars and turns to Brad.

                    LARRY
         There's a roll of duct-tape in the glove
         compartment. Could you grab it for me?

INT. BRAD'S HOUSE, HALLWAY — NIGHT

Brad closes the front door removes his shoes, and makes his way on
soft feet up the stairway. One of the stairs creaks. He cringes.

                    KATHY (O.C.)
         Honey?

He's busted.

                    BRAD
              (like a teenager)
         ....hi.

BRAD & KATHY'S BEDROOM

                    KATHY
         Where were you?

Brad stands in the doorway, and musters what bravado he can.

                    BRAD
         I, uh, joined this group, the *Committee of
         Concerned Parents*. We're distributing
         flyers about that creep on Woodward Court.

She stares at him: his torn collar, scraped knees, scratched cheek, and
sweat-stained armpits.

>   KATHY
>   (concerned)
>   Were you attacked?

>   BRAD
>   These guys play a little touch football
>   after.

>   KATHY
>   This late?

>   BRAD
>   ...it's a night league.

Kathy looks confused.

>   KATHY
>   So it's going to be a regular thing?

>   BRAD
>   No...just once a week, after I'm finished
>   at the library. That okay?

>   KATHY
>   Who are the guys?

>   BRAD
>   (gaining momentum)
>   You remember Larry Hedges from the
>   sprinkler park? The guy with the twins?
>   It's his organization.

>   KATHY
>   I thought you didn't like him.

>   BRAD
>   He's okay. But this committee makes a lot
>   of sense. It's pretty scary having a guy
>   like that living right by the playground.

Kathy gazes lovingly at Aaron.

>   KATHY
>   I know. I hate to even think about it.

She looks back up at her husband.

>   KATHY
>   Well, you better take a shower.

INT. BRAD'S BATHROOM — NIGHT

Brad's in the shower, frantically soaping himself.

>   VOICE
>   Brad showered quickly, sensing a rare
>   opportunity to have sex with his wife.

Brad brushes his teeth at twice the normal speed.

                    VOICE
          This is just what I need, he thought.
          Something to take my mind off that kiss.

INT. BRAD'S BEDROOM — NIGHT

He emerges from the bathroom, wearing only boxers and his most
romantic smile. He crosses to the bed and places his hands under
Aaron, preparing to transfer him to his own room.

                    KATHY
          Please don't.

                    BRAD
               (trying to stay calm)
          Come on, Kathy. How many times do we have
          to argue about this? He needs to start
          sleeping by himself.

                    KATHY
          I know. But he just looks so comfy.

                    BRAD
          He'll be just as comfy in his own bed.

                    KATHY
          I know...I just miss him so much.

                    BRAD
          I'm getting a little tired of waking up
          with his foot in my face.

                    KATHY
          But it's a perfect foot. Look at him.
          Just look at him.

Brad ponders his sleeping child.

                    BRAD
          He is a handsome devil.

                    KATHY
          He's perfect.

Brad sighs and climbs into bed. Before turning off the light, Kathy
leans over Aaron to give him a kiss.

                    KATHY
          Good night.

                    BRAD
          Good night.

EXT. SARAH'S HOUSE — DAY

A formidable colonial on a hilly double lot.

                    VOICE
          Number two Hillcrest was an impressive
          piece of real estate.

INT. SARAH'S HOUSE, VARIOUS EMPTY ROOMS — SAME

Space and windows. A beautiful floor plan, somewhat grand. Looking around you will notice a kind of dead beauty to the place. All dressed up and no place to go.

> VOICE
> Even so, Sarah was ambivalent about the house that she occupied. She wasn't involved with it's purchase or design. The place was a hand-me-down of sorts from Richard's mother, and the furnishings were left-overs from his first marriage.

INT. SARAH'S HOUSE, UPSTAIRS ATTIC UTILITY ROOM — SAME

A small dark narrow space with a single window at the end. An old MATTRESS & BOX SPRINGS rest against the wall.

> VOICE
> By the time Sarah arrived here, Richard wasn't all that interested in redecorating. And so she decided to leave it as it was...

A YOUNGER and VERY PREGNANT SARAH sorts through a gaggle of moving boxes adorned with her name. She lifts out stack after stack of BOOKS.

INT. SARAH'S DOWNSTAIRS STUDY — DAY

Shelves full of books. From highbrow to lowbrow: Faulkner, Yates, Dubus, Diet, Feminine Literature, Romantic Poets, Stein, Tuscany, Travel, White, Whitman, Wolff, and *What's Your Birth sign?* — seasons in a reader's life.

> VOICE
> ...with the exception of a single room that she staked out for her own, and gradually began to populate it with the remnants of her former self.

Sarah, wearing reading glasses, sits at a writing table situated directly under a window, transcribing passages from *Working With Feminist Criticism* by Mary Eagleton. She makes notes into a MT. TOM 6X4 NOTEBOOK from BOB SLATE.

Lucy, carrying her own book, wanders over and stares up at her mother. Sarah is oblivious.

> LUCY
> Read me story.

> SARAH
> In a minute.

Lucy pulls at Sarah's notebook.

> LUCY
> I sit on your lap.

Sarah pulls back.

                         SARAH
              I said in a minute. Now go on, finish
              your program. Go.

The child retreats. Sarah returns to her studies.

                         VOICE
              From the moment Lucy was born, Sarah had
              refused to hire someone for child care.
              She wasn't exactly sure why she had taken
              this stance. The truth was she spent most
              afternoons marking time...

Sarah glances impatiently at her watch.

She spots a toy left behind by Lucy — She rises from the writing
table, bends down to pick up the item, moves to the doorway, and
places it on a side-table outside the room. She steps back into her
study, and closes the door.

                         VOICE
              ...waiting desperately for the moment when
              her husband returned from work and she
              could finally have a moment to herself.
              But even this was not something she could
              rely on.

INT. SARAH'S FRONT ENTRY WAY — MAGIC

Sarah opens the door to reveal JEAN, a vigorous 60 year-old woman,
pumping her arms and legs on the front stoop.

                         JEAN
              Ready to roll?

                         SARAH
              Could you wait a few minutes? Richard's
              barricaded in the upstairs office
              finishing up some stuff for work.

                         JEAN
              No problem. I have a little surprise for
              someone anyway.

Jean steps into the house.

                         SARAH
              She's a terror tonight. I couldn't get
              her to nap again.

                         JEAN
              Poor thing.

                         SARAH
              Poor Mommy is more like it.

Sarah closes the front door.

INT. SARAH'S FRONT ENTRY WAY — CONTINUOUS

Jean cups her hands around her mouth.

                         JEAN
             Hellooo? Is there a cute little girl in
             the house?

LUCY runs in from the other room, jumps up and throws herself into
the older woman's arms as if they're lovers meeting in an airport.

Jean rotates her JUMBO FANNY PACK and tugs slowly on the zipper.

                         JEAN
             Oh my goodness. Look what I found.

With the flair of a magician, Jean produces a TINY STUFFED DOG from
the pouch and hands it to an awestruck Lucy.

                         LUCY
             A Beanie!

                         SARAH
             Jean, you didn't have to do that.

                         JEAN
             This dog needed a little girl to take
             care of him. And I knew a little girl who
             needed a dog.

                         LUCY
             Thank you, Jean.

INT. SARAH'S STUDY — LATER (MAGIC)

Sarah sits at her writing table, her impatience growing by the second.
LUCY & JEAN play in the next room at the kitchen table. Sarah extends
her leg, and gently closes the door. She turns and We MOVE IN on her
annoyed face -

                         VOICE
             Sarah was beginning to get angry. Her
             evening fitness walk was the one thing
             she looked forward to all day, and
             Richard knew this. She didn't care how
             busy he was, it was a simple matter of
             equity.

INT. SARAH'S HOUSE, UPSTAIRS OFFICE — SAME

A SILVER-FRAMED PHOTOGRAPH of Sarah and Lucy rests on a desk.

A distinguished looking MAN in his mid-forties sits behind the desk,
focusing on the COMPUTER SCREEN in front of him.

                         VOICE
             If there was one thing life had taught
             Richard, it was that it was ridiculous to
             be at war with your own desires.

RICHARD opens his desk drawer and removes a small rectangular UPS
shipping box.

                         VOICE
             He could easily imagine what people would
             say if they could see him now...

With trembling hands, he breaks the seal on the box, and withdraws a
MANILA ENVELOPE decorated with STICKERS, RED HEARTS and STARS.

                         VOICE
            ...exactly the same thing they'd say if
            someone had told them that Ray...

Richard glances at A BOX that appears over HIS RIGHT SHOULDER. In it
— RAY, a man in his 30s, dressed in sweats, under-hands a ball to his
son who swings for a hit.

                         VOICE
            ...from next door was a transvestite...

Alone now, in Ray's imagined bedroom, he gazes into a MIRROR applying LI
STICK.

                         VOICE
            ...or that Ted from work had anonymous
            gay sex at highway rest stops.

Richard glances at A NEW BOX that appears over HIS LEFT SHOULDER. In
it — another man, TED, stands at a bank of URINALS, he gives a side-
long glance to a SKINNY MAN using the next one over.

As Richard looks back down at the envelope in his hands the BOXES
disappear. Richard takes out a LETTER OPENER and slices through the
packing tape on the envelope.

                         VOICE
            But we want what we want, Richard
            thought, and there's not much we can do
            about it.

Before removing the contents of the envelope, Richard takes the
photograph of his wife and daughter and turns it face down on the
desk.

INT. RICHARD'S PLACE OF BUSINESS — DAY — ELEVEN MONTHS AGO

                         VOICE
            He had stumbled on the site eleven months
            ago, while doing research for a
            consulting firm.

A SQUARE ROOM with dozens of MANNED CUBICLES, through the maze on the
other side of the place is -

A 600 square-foot office with a window, where —

RICHARD sits at his desk, his attention focused on his FLAT-SCREEN.

                         VOICE
            His office door was wide open.

Richard glances up from the monitor furtively.

He takes a breath, and his eyes go back to the monitor.

His HAND holding the MOUSE hovers with anticipation.

                              VOICE
             But he clicked on the link anyway.

ON the MONITOR is the HOMEPAGE of SLUTTY KAY, a BLONDE WOMAN, in her
thirties. There's something graphically homegrown about the design.
It looks authentic, and not put together by a consortium in Glendale.
In large friendly quotes it says *"actively pursuing a swinging
lifestyle, and my God-given sexuality."*

His hand moves the mouse. The cursor clicks on *Read More About Me.* A
long Q & A appears next to a new image of Kay bending over a table.
She wears a SHORT TARTAN SKIRT with NO PANTIES.

                              VOICE
             He was deeply engrossed in his discovery
             when Ted knocked on his door...

TED, Richard's imagined REST STOP CRUISER stands in the doorway.

                              VOICE
             ...taking orders for a lunch run.

Richard looks up.

                              VOICE
             Casually, but with great haste,

Richard's hand invisibly moves his mouse.

                              VOICE
             Richard banished Slutty Kay from his
             screen...

Kay's homepage collapses, the monitor now shows a spread sheet of
another kind.

                              VOICE
             ...told Ted that he'd like a Chicken
             Caesar...

Ted nods, and departs.

                              VOICE
             ...and re-entered the flow of an ordinary
             day...

Richard refers to some papers, and inputs data into his machine.

                              VOICE
             ...it wasn't until several months later
             that Richard gave the slightest thought
             to the site he had stumbled upon...

INT. RICHARD'S PLACE OF BUSINESS — NIGHT — SEVERAL MONTHS LATER

The overhead lights are off for the night. The only illumination in
the place emanating from an office on the other side of the room,
where —

RICHARD sits at his desk, shuffling papers, pretending to be busy. A
middle-aged SECRETARY pokes her head into the room.

                         SECRETARY
          Do you need me for anything else?

                          RICHARD
          No, why don't you head home? I'm gonna
          catch up on some e-mail.

                         SECRETARY
          Well, don't stay too late. Your dinner'll
          get cold.

Richard smiles and waves goodbye. He lets a couple of seconds pass,
then gets up and locks his office door.

Richard returns to his desk, his attention now refocused on his flat-
screen.

                           VOICE
          Lately, Slutty Kay had become a problem.

The cursor highlights a BOOKMARK in his preferences entitled —
Slutty Kay positions & implements.

                           VOICE
          He thought about her far too often, and
          spent hours studying the thousands of
          photographs available to him.

Richard's CURSOR flies across the SCREEN and launches his BROWSER.

Kay appears in various positions, outfits, and as the bookmark title
indicated, utilizing all kinds of implements.

                           VOICE
          Some of Kay's practices struck him as
          bizarre, even off-putting. She had a
          thing about kitchen utensils, spatulas,
          barbecue forks, and dressing up like a
          little girl and playing with balloons.
          But who was Richard to judge?

He pulls a box of KLEENEX from the BOTTOM DRAWER, and licks his lips.
His eyes dreamy, and hungry. He pulls down his trousers and gets down
to business.

                           VOICE
          Though, as close as Richard sometimes
          felt to Slutty Kay — as much as he
          believed that he *knew* her...

Richard keeps yanking, a desperate impatience on his face.

                           VOICE
          ...he could never get past the
          uncomfortable fact that she existed for
          him solely as a digital image.

He looks down at his lap. Things don't seem to be going well.

INT. SARAH'S HOUSE, UPSTAIRS OFFICE — BACK TO PRESENT — MAGIC

CLOSE ON: Richard's HANDS as they remove the contents of the HEART-COVERED MANILA ENVELOPE: three POLAROIDS of SLUTTY KAY wearing a POLKA DOT THONG in various poses. Each of them bear the greeting, scrawled in black sharpie, *Hi Richard!*

                    VOICE
          The panties were an attempt to solve this
          problem.

His HANDS reach back in and pull out the actual THONG in the photos. He raises it a couple of inches from his face, tentatively giving it his nasal appraisal.

                    VOICE
          Maybe a sniff or two would hurry things
          along, so he could get back downstairs to
          his real life...

He reaches down with his other hand, and jerks off.

                    VOICE
          ... where his wife and daughter were
          waiting for him, their impatience
          increasing by the minute.

SARAH stands at the bottom of the stairway staring up. Her patience at an end. She hesitates just a moment before making the long climb. Unaware that she is about to play her own version of Aaron's *Train Wreck.*

She arrives outside the office door, and gives a tentative knock. No answer. She reaches down and turns the knob. The door swings open to —

RICHARD jerking. He now wears the polka dot thong like a gas mask: over his mouth and nose. Inhaling its scent with gusto.

SARAH peers inside. Her expression wavering between revulsion and amazement. Richard is oblivious.

                    SARAH
          Ahem.

Richard whips his head around, the thong still pressed over the lower half of his face. He scrambles to hide the evidence.

                    SARAH
          Is this going to take much longer? I'd
          really like to go for my walk.

                    RICHARD
               (pulling the thong off his face)
          You could have knocked.

                    SARAH
          I did.
               (backing out of the room)
          We need to talk.

SARAH'S STREET — MAGIC

Sarah and Jean at the end of their power walk.

> JEAN
> You're awfully quiet tonight. Everything
> okay?

Sarah snaps out of it.

> SARAH
> What? Yeah.

> JEAN
> You'll have to walk without me tomorrow
> night. I have a book group meeting.

> SARAH
> Okay.

Silence. Then.

> JEAN
> You're sure everything's alright?

> SARAH
> Yeah, sorry, I guess I'm just a little
> tired... so, what are you reading?

> JEAN
> *Crime and Punishment.*

> SARAH
> Wow. That's pretty highbrow for a book
> group.

They turn the final corner onto their own street.

> JEAN
> We have some very stimulating
> discussions. You should come next month.
> We're doing *Madame Bovary.* You could be
> my little sister.

> SARAH
> Little sister?

> JEAN
> We're trying to get younger women
> involved. We call them our little
> sisters.

> SARAH
> I don't know. I read *Madame Bovary* in
> grad school. It's a pretty misogynist
> text.

Sarah slows, squinting at a shadowy figure on her front steps.

                    JEAN
          Well, that's an interesting perspective.
          You should come.

                    SARAH
          Excuse me, Jean. Someone's at my door.
          I'll call you.

Sarah hurries off, leaving Jean behind in the street.

THERESA from the playground sits on Sarah's front steps, smoking a
cigarette. She smiles stiffly as Sarah approaches.

Sarah stops at the base of the steps.

                    SARAH
               (a bit flustered)
          Well, this is a surprise. I haven't seen
          you since...

                    THERESA
          I hope you don't mind. Your husband said
          you'd be back any minute.

                    SARAH
          Not at all.

She smiles at Theresa.

                    SARAH
          It's good to see you. Can I make you a
          cup of tea or something?

                    THERESA
          I can only stay a minute. I just wanted
          to warn you. You know that guy? The
          pervert? He's been riding his bike near
          the playground, checking out the kids.

                    SARAH
          Oh, God. Do the police know?

                    THERESA
          Nothing they can do. He's not breaking
          any laws. I guess they're waiting for him
          to kill someone. I just thought you
          should know.

                    SARAH
          Thanks. That's nice of you.
               (then, plaintively)
          You sure you don't want some tea?

                    THERESA
          I'm sorry.

Theresa stands up.

                    THERESA
          I don't think it's a good idea.

                         SARAH
                    (after a beat)
          I didn't mean to kiss him. I don't even
          know how it happened.

She pats Sarah gently on the arm.

                         THERESA
          I better go. Mike's gonna worry.

She leaves Sarah standing there alone. Sarah turns and stares at the
front door, stealing herself for what she knows is waiting for her on
the other side. She lets out a groan, reaches for the doorknob and
heads into -

INT. SARAH'S HOUSE, FOYER — SAME

The front entry-way, where Richard stands wearing a hangdog expression.
He stares at her pathetically, like a child waiting to be forgiven.

                         RICHARD
          ...you want to talk?

Sarah brushes past him and heads upstairs.

                         SARAH
          I'm tired.

Richard looks both disappointed and relieved.

INT. SARAH'S HOUSE, UPSTAIRS HALLWAY — MORNING

Sarah peeks into Lucy's room. The child is still asleep. THE SOUND OF
A CAR STARTING brings Sarah over to the window at the top of the
stairs. She looks down at —

THE DRIVEWAY

To see Richard's car pulling away, on his way to work.

UPSTAIRS OFFICE

Sarah closes the door to Richard's office, moves over to the window,
pulls up the shade, and scans the room. She moves over to the desk,
and begins to investigate — looking at paperwork, rifling drawers,
and examining computer disks. She glances down at a small WASTEBASKET
topped with WADDED UP TISSUES. She grimaces, disgusted.

INT. BRAD'S HOUSE, DINING ROOM — SAME

Brad sits at the dining room table going through credit card bills
from five different companies. A YELLOW POST IT is attached to the
outside of one of the envelopes. In a neat feminine cursive is
scrawled "Brad! Please look this over." His hands obey, and pull out
an itemized report, that has multiple items highlighted *Sports
illustrated, Men's Fitness,* and *Mothering Magazine*. In the margins
the same cursive asks "Do you really need these?" The phone rings,
and Brad answers it.

                              BRAD
                Hello? No, he's still sleeping...yeah,
                I'm going through them now...No, I guess
                I don't need them...alright have a good —

She's already hung up. Brad hangs up, closes his eyes, and steels
himself. He looks utterly defeated.

SARAH'S STUDY — MOMENTS LATER

AN UNTOUCHED MUG OF TEA on the writing table in front of her, Sarah
sits there with a thousand mile stare on her face. Finally, she picks
up her notebook, and book of essays on *Feminist Criticism*, and tries
to get interested. It's no use. She sets them down abruptly, and
moves over to —

A SIDE-TABLE stacked with periodicals. She rifles through and
discards: *Ad Busters, Mother Jones, The Utne Reader, The Paris
Review,* before finding the object of her desire — the latest
catalogue from J-CREW.

She moves to an old HIGH-BACK CHAIR with her prize, and starts
browsing the pages. She takes a huge gulp of tea, her left hand
absently reaches for the television remote, and turns on the set.
An infomercial for *Nature-Bra* preaches "the joys of perky breasts."
Sarah focuses on a J-CREW Model clad in a RED ONE PIECE BATHING
SUIT, as the seductive spokeswoman for *Nature-Bra* points out the
possible benefits of using this product "post breast feeding." Sarah
turns her attention from the catalogue to the screen, just in time
to "learn how to order."

EXT. SARAH'S HOUSE — MORNING

A FED-EX TRUCK pulls away after making it's appointed rounds.

INT. SARAH'S HOUSE, KITCHEN TABLE — DAY

A KITCHEN KNIFE rips through a CARDBOARD BOX past a shipping label
from J-CREW.

EXT. TOWN POOL — DAY

Wearing an unbuttoned MEN'S SHIRT over her BATHING SUIT, Sarah peers
through a CHAIN-LINK FENCE, Lucy at her side.

An enormous rectangle of water framed by a CONCRETE WALKWAY, set at
the bottom of a grassy hill.

A SLY SMILE OF RECOGNITION passes across Sarah's face.

In the middle-distance BRAD AND AARON SIT SHADED BY A TREE.

Sarah flashes her ID at a BORED-LOOKING TEENAGER reading a Stephen
King novel. The kid waves them in. Sarah takes Lucy straight to

THE WADING POOL. She attaches a pair of INFLATABLE WATER-WINGS to
Lucy's arms, and sits her on the edge of the pool. She sneaks a
glance up the hill toward Brad & Aaron's tree, hoping to catch a
certain someone's eye. She does.

BRAD, shirtless, sits on a beach towel in a patch of shade. He looks
in her direction. Then looks away quickly.

SARAH sets LUCY into the WADING POOL, and makes a show of playing with her daughter, throwing the occasional glance up the hill to make sure he's still there -

He is, pretending to read a magazine.. Aaron in his JESTER'S CAP, stages collisions with TOY TRUCKS. But the boy grows bored and toddles over to his father, pulling on Brad's arm.

                    AARON
          Daddy. I go in pool now.

Brad's not sure he's ready for that.

                    BRAD
          ...in a minute.

                    AARON
          Daddy, now!

IN THE WADING POOL, Sarah watches Lucy, but she's clearly distracted. She steals another look.

                    LUCY
          Mommy? I havta to go pee pee.

                    SARAH
          Just go in the pool.

Lucy shakes her head *no*.

                    SARAH
          Really? Okay, c'mon.

She grabs Lucy, and they head to the LADIES'S LOCKER ROOM.

UNDER THE TREE, Brad sees his chance to avoid an encounter, and satisfy Aaron at the same time. He stands, picks up his son, and heads down the hill toward the pool.

IN THE WADING POOL, Brad & Aaron roughhouse and play. Brad is more engaged with his child, but like Sarah, he can't help wishing he had eyes in the back of his head. He keeps scanning the area, on the lookout for her. His eyes fixate on the LADIES'S LOCKER ROOM DOOR. Women and children come and go, but no Sarah or Lucy.

Finally Brad begins to relax, allowing himself to become completely absorbed in play.

LATER

Brad and Aaron squint into the sun as they trudge up the hill toward their tree. It's not until they have almost reached the shady place that they discover —

SARAH & LUCY spread out on towels right next to their own.

                    SARAH
               (mock surprise)
          Oh my God, it's you.

Brad stares at her, somewhat surprised, and worried at the same time.

                         BRAD
          Wow. Hey.

Sarah removes a BOTTLE OF SUNSCREEN from a bag. She squeezes a gob of
it into her hand and begins slathering it all over Lucy, who submits
like a good soldier. She turns to Brad.

                         SARAH
          I hope you don't mind. Lucy has sensitive
          skin. She's better off in the shade.

                         BRAD
                    (polite)
          Not at all. It's nice to see you again.

He sets Aaron down on their blanket, and begins drying the boy off.

After finishing with Lucy, Sarah removes the MEN'S SHIRT; revealing
her RED ONE PIECE. She begins to rub lotion on her arms.

                         SARAH
                    (casually)
          I'm sorry, could you get my back?

Brad turns around.

                         BRAD
          ...um, okay, sure.

He squirts lotion into his hand and begins RUBBING IT INTO HER BACK
in a POLITE and BUSINESSLIKE MANNER. Sarah closes her eyes and leans
back into the massage. After a few seconds, she smiles over her
shoulder.

                         SARAH
          Thanks alot. Lucy? Say hi to the little
          boy from the playground.

                         LUCY
          Hi.

                         ARRON
          Hi.

                         SARAH
          Remember him?

                         VOICE
          The pool became a ritual.

EXT. TOWN POOL — ANOTHER DAY

Sarah & Lucy arrive at the entrance. Sarah waves to Brad who has
already arrived, and sits with Aaron under the tree. He waves back.

                         VOICE
          Day after day, they sat together in the
          shade, getting to know each other...

Same spot, DIFFERENT DAY. Now Sarah's doing Brad's back.

                              VOICE
                    distributing snacks...

SARAH DISBURSES GOLDFISH CRACKERS TO EACH CHILD

                              VOICE
                    ...and brokering occasional disputes.

AARON AND LUCY ENGAGE IN A FIERCE STRUGGLE FOR POSSESSION OF ONE OF
SARAH'S FLIP FLOPS

                              VOICE
                    Having little choice in the matter, Aaron
                    and Lucy formed a fragile friendship.

LUCY LISTENS TO BIG BEAR'S HEART WITH A TOY STETHOSCOPE. AARON
ADMINISTERS AN INJECTION WITH A TOY SYRINGE

                              VOICE
                    Sometimes Brad and Sarah traded
                    offspring.

IN THE POOL, BRAD TEACHES LUCY HOW TO DOG-PADDLE

ON THE BLANKET, SARAH HOLDS A SLEEPY AARON IN HER ARMS, HIS HEAD ON HER
SHOULDER, THE TENDRILS OF HIS HEADGEAR DROOPING OVER HER BACK AND CHEST.
HER FACE BREAKS INTO A GRIN AS...

...MARY ANN, wearing SUNGLASSES AND A FLOPPY HAT, spots her from the
walkway. Mary Ann puts on a painfully fake smile and waves to Sarah.

Sarah waves back triumphantly.

                              VOICE
                    It was the most fun Sarah had had in
                    years.

Fresh from the pool, Brad leans back and soaks up the sun, his body
glistening with luminous droplets of water.

Sarah devours him with her eyes.

                              VOICE
                    But there was always that longing to
                    touch, to be touched by Brad. And as
                    badly as she wanted this, she wanted just
                    as badly to hold on to the innocent
                    public life they'd made for themselves
                    out in the open, with the other parents
                    and children.

DAMP AND TIRED, BRAD AND SARAH GATHER UP THEIR THINGS.

                              VOICE
                    So she accepted the trade...

With a bittersweet expression, Brad extends his hand to Sarah.

                              VOICE
                    ...the melancholy handshake at four
                    o'clock...

They shake and part ways.

                    VOICE
          ...in exchange for this little patch of
          grass, some sunscreen and companionship.

Late light rakes an empty pool, and its now deserted surroundings.

                    VOICE
          One more happy day at the pool.

INT. BRAD'S HOUSE, KITCHEN — MORNING

Aaron sits in his highchair shovelling oatmeal into his mouth. Kathy
marks up some copy with a red pen as she finishes with her breakfast.
Brad watches the two of them, waiting to be noticed or acknowledged
in some way, shape, or form. Finally, Kathy speaks.

                    KATHY
          No pasta for dinner, okay? We eat way too
          much pasta around here.

                    BRAD
          I thought you liked pasta.

                    KATHY
          I do. That's the problem. Pretty soon
          I'll be able to sell advertising space on
          my ass... I better hurry. I've got a nine
          o'clock at TAPS.

She rises, gathers up paperwork and the breakfast plates.

                    BRAD
          What is that?

                    KATHY
          Tragedy Assistance Program for Survivors.

                    BRAD
          I thought you were already editing.

She carries the dishes over to the sink.

                    KATHY
          So did I. But this family's story just
          got me... the father was killed in a
          mortar attack on his base. Left behind a
          a little boy, and a baby girl.

She starts rinsing plates.

                    KATHY
          I spoke with his wife on the phone
          yesterday... said she didn't know what
          she was gonna do next Christmas.

                    BRAD
          Oh jeez, I bet.

She shakes her head.

                         KATHY
                    (reflective)
          No, it wasn't like that. It was more
          wondering if she should keep a tradition
          with her son that she began with the boy's
          father... said her husband had had a knack
          for requesting odd Christmas gifts. A scuba
          suit one year, rappelling gear the
          next...said he wasn't afraid to try
          anything.

Over Brad's face — THE NOON BELLS TOLL FROM ST. PAUL'S TOWER.

EXT. TOWN POOL — DAY

It's hot, humid, and horrible. The children sit together on a towel
occupied with their play. Sarah lies on her back BRAD'S T-SHIRT over
her face.

Brad allows himself the pleasure of pouring his eyes over Sarah's
body completely unobserved. Then —

                         SARAH
          Hot enough for you?

For a moment, Brad thinks he's been caught, but then he realizes it's
an innocent enough question.

                         BRAD
          ...yeah, it's so humid. I got Football
          practice tonight. Be like playing in a
          sauna.

                         SARAH
          Watch out for that Italian guy. What's
          his name again?

                         BRAD
          Correnti?

Brad smiles, pleased that she's taken an interest, and has even gone
so far as to remember something he only mentioned in passing.

                         SARAH
          Yeah. Remember what happened to your knee
          last week?

She lays the back of her hand surreptitiously on his chest.

                         SARAH
          You should be careful, Brad.

He stares at her hand just as she moves it away.

                         BRAD
          I'll be careful.

                         SARAH
          Promise?

                              BRAD
                           (smiles)
                    Yeah. Yeah, I promise

A moment passes between them.

Brad breaks it by talking about - what else? The weather.

                              BRAD
                       (looks at the sky)
                    Weatherman said scattered showers. I
                    don't see any scattered showers.

A man in LOUD SWIM TRUNKS, with an ORANGE DIVING MASK on his forehead
and a SCUBA FLIPPER in each hand, stands by the lifeguard chair. He
scans his surroundings. He is —

The face from the flyers, RONNIE MCGORVEY.

McGorvey drops his towel and begins putting on his flippers.

He lowers his mask, slides feet-first into the pool, and begins
exploring — participating in water play, and taking in the general
scenery.

SARAH props her self up and reaches for her book. It is at precisely
this moment that she sees him.

                              SARAH
                    Oh my God.

                              BRAD
                    What?

                              SARAH
                    It's him.

                              BRAD
                           (squinting)
                    Oh, Jesus.

At first, no one else seems to notice his presence in the water.
BEACH BALLS float through the air. Kids keep CANNONBALLING and BELLY-
FLOPPING off the diving board.

But then, not far from Brad and Sarah on the hill, an EXTREMELY
AGITATED WOMAN stands up, and shouts.

                         AGITATED WOMAN
                    Jimmy! Jimmy Mancino! Out of the pool
                    this instant!

A SKINNY TEN-YEAR-OLD starts paddling uncertainly toward the edge of
the pool.

                         AGITATED WOMAN
                    Jimmy, now!

ANOTHER ADULT VOICE rings out, followed by a PARENTAL CHORUS.

ADULT VOICE
Randall, Juliette! You too!

PARENTAL CHORUS
Grace! Pablo! Ruby! Tyler! Max! Rebecca!
Lilly! Zoe!

The SHALLOW END empties first, ANXIOUS MOTHERS wading out with FRIGHTENED TODDLERS in their arms. Before long, the OLDER KIDS are climbing out, too, standing in sullen confusion on the walkway.

All over the hillside, adults are whipping out MOBILE PHONES, dialing 911.

UNDERWATER - Ronnie McGorvey plunges toward the bottom of the deep end with the heavy grace of a seal. He rises slowly -

Breaking the SURFACE to find himself alone in the pool.

Ronnie's EYES dart around inside his MASK, absorbing the situation.

He ducks BACK UNDER, cutting through the water, moving his arms in wide lazy circles. He looks peaceful, unhurried.

He FLOATS on his BACK for a while, his pale belly rising out of the water like a deserted island.

MINUTES LATER

TWO COPS enter the pool area and approach McGorvey. Aaron and Lucy have taken notice, too.

LUCY
Why the police is here?

Sarah checks with Brad, uncertain.

SARAH
There's a man in the pool that didn't buy
a ticket to get in, and the police are
asking him to leave.

The cops speak to McGorvey. The exchange seems polite, almost friendly. After a moment, one cop reaches down and gives him a hand getting out of the water.

AARON
What's those? On the feet?

BRAD
Flippers. They help you swim better.

McGorvey grabs his towel, and begins trudging toward the exit, his flippers slapping wetly on the ground. He stops to pull them off, then strips off the mask, turning toward the hillside. He spreads his arms wide, addressing the public in a loud voice.

MCGORVEY
I was only trying to cool off!

EXT. TOWN POOL — LATER

It seems like the whole town has crowded into the pool, the DECENT
PEOPLE OF East Wyndam reclaiming it for their own.

The COLLECTIVE FUNK has broken. Adults get into giggly splashing
fights. Everybody tries to keep a beach ball aloft.

THE SUN BEGINS TO DISAPPEAR BEHIND A CLOUD.

The DISTANT RUMBLE of THUNDER. The sky goes DARK. It begins to SHOWER.

It seems like good fun until the LIGHTNING FLASH. A LIFEGUARD speaks
through a LOUDSPEAKER.

                    LIFEGUARD (O.C.)
          Clear the pool, please.

The rain intensifies as Sarah and Brad gather their things.

A SAVAGE CRACK OF THUNDER SOUNDS. Lucy whimpers and latches onto
Sarah's leg. Sarah lifts her up.

                    SARAH
          We better get going.

                    BRAD
          You're gonna carry her?

                    SARAH
          It'll be faster.

                    BRAD
          That's crazy. Put her in the stroller.

Sarah glances at the stroller. BIG BEAR stares back.

                    SARAH
          She won't do the stroller.

                    BRAD
          Hey, Lucy? Want a ride?

Lucy unlatches from Sarah's leg and runs right into Brad's arms, and
he sets her up in the thing.

Sarah is both impressed, and envious.

                    SARAH
          But it's out of your way.

                    BRAD
          We don't mind, do we, Aaron?

A FLASH OF LIGHTNING

                    SARAH
          Okay. Then run, quick.

EXT. SARAH'S STREET — LATER

Brad pushes the double stroller at a fast clip. Sarah, carrying Big Bear in her arms, leads him toward her house.

EXT. SARAH'S HOUSE (SUN ROOM) — SAME

Sarah kneels down to unbuckle Lucy. Both kids SLEEP LIKE ANGELS, Lucy's head lolling on Aaron's shoulder.

Sarah hesitates, uncertain whether to invite Brad in. This AWKWARD MOMENT is interrupted by a CLOSE LIGHTNING FLASH.

                    SARAH
          You better come in. I can't let you walk
          home in this.

INT. SARAH'S HOUSE, LIVING ROOM, STAIRS — SAME

The two enter with the kids in tow. Sarah heads straight in, Brad a few paces behind, takes in the place: Expensive, tasteful, and a couple of notches up the food chain from what he is used to. Sarah heads upstairs carrying Lucy.

                    SARAH
          We can lie them down in Lucy's room.

                    BRAD
          Okay.

He follows her up the stairway.

INT. LUCY'S BEDROOM — DAY

The children, dry now, sleep on Lucy's bed. AARON clad in one of LUCY'S FLOWER COVERED NIGHTGOWNS. Brad and Sarah, still soaked, watch them in nervous silence.

                    SARAH
               (whispers)
          This is amazing. She never naps.

                    BRAD
               (whispers)
          Aaron'll be out for the next two hours.
          I'll have to get him out of that
          nightgown before he wakes up, or he'll
          never forgive me.

Sarah looks at him and smiles.

UPSTAIRS HALLWAY — MOMENTS LATER

Brad waits on the stairs as Sarah secures the BABY GATE.

BOTTOM OF STAIRS/LIVINGROOM - SAME

Sarah & Brad head down the final stairs, and into the living room. The safety of the public arena removed, makes keeping each other's company clumsy.

                    BRAD
          Nice place.

                    SARAH
          You think so?

                    BRAD
          Yeah.

                    SARAH
          Richard does alright for himself.

The comment is not meant to intimidate, but it does.

                    BRAD
          What's he do again?

                    SARAH
          Lies.

They stand there staring at each other. Puddles forming at their
feet.

                    SARAH
          Um. Please, have a seat. Make yourself at
          home.

Brad laughs, and pulls at his soaked clothing.

                    BRAD
          I better not. I'll ruin your furniture.

                    SARAH
               (nervous)
          Right. I'll just put the children's
          things in the dryer, and get us some
          towels.

She heads out of the room quickly, leaving Brad alone.

He looks off the main entry way to a succession of small rooms, an
open door leads to the first room situated behind a back staircase,
clearly what was at one time quarters for a maid. He steps inside.
Nothing much to see. On the other side of the room is another door,
slightly ajar. He wanders in that direction, and opens the door,
finding —

SARAH'S STUDY

He steps into the room, and takes a quick inventory of the place, *her*
place.

He moves toward her old high-back, and pushes a finger into one of
the many holes in its torn fabric.

One of SARAH'S SCARVES is draped across the top of the chair. He
places his palm underneath the garment — the material cascading over
his hand.

At the base of a VASE full of FRESH FLOWERS lie Sarah's READING
GLASSES.

The tips of his fingers glide across her writing table, past *Theresa Raquin,* to a book of *English Love Sonnets.* The book opens easily, marked by an, as yet, not fully dry rose, pressed against an oft read piece: Sonnet 147 by William Shakespeare. Specific lines appear to have been recently underlined:

My Love is as a fever, The uncertain sickly appetite to please, Angry that his prescriptions are not kept, Past cure am I.

He turns the page to find a tucked-in SNAP-SHOT of BRAD, AARON, and LUCY at the town pool.

The book snaps shut.

He puts it back down on the table, like it may burn his hand.

His face a mess of conflicting emotions.

LAUNDRY ROOM - SAME

Sarah empties dry bedding and towels from a FRONT LOADER into an empty laundry basket. She grabs the children's wet things, throws them into the dryer and starts the cycle. She moves the basket to a folding table on the other side of the small basement room, pulls out two towels and begins folding them into thirds.

Slowly, A SHADOW begins to grow across her back —

Brad's shoulder, and head appear.

She continues folding. Oblivious to everything but the sound of the dryer.

He raises his hand, about to place it on her arm, when suddenly she turns, coming face-to-face with him. Startled, she gasps.

She looks genuinely frightened. What is he doing down here?

The two of them just stare at each other — both appear unable to move. Finally, she lifts up the two towels she has folded, and offers one to him, there is something oddly formal about her gesture.

He takes the towel from her hand and drops it to the floor. She somewhat timidly drops the other one.

He pulls her into him, and begins to kiss her, gentle, then forceful.

Her eyes dart all over the place. Then instinct kick in, and she surrenders to the moment. The kiss becomes completely electrifying, the kind of kiss that would make perfect sense outside a dorm room at two in the morning. Their hands find each other for the first time, all bets are off — the play is real.

LAUNDRY ROOM — MOMENTS LATER

SQUAUK — The dryer announces that it has reached the end of its cycle. However, the silence is short-lived. Grateful moans accompany the view of Sarah perched on the edge of a STONE SOAP SINK, gripping Brad's backside as he thrusts himself into her.

Brad picks up the pace. They've reached a level of near-frenzy, when Brad SUDDENLY STOPS.

> BRAD
> Do you feel guilty about this?

Sarah thinks this over.

> SARAH
> No. I don't.

> BRAD
> I do. I feel really bad.

Sarah grimaces, steeling herself for disappointment. But the deliberate motion of Brad's body betray his words, putting her mind at ease, and her body on high alert. She begins to vocalize uncontrollably. The laundry room door is slightly open, and she looks toward the -

HALLWAY

Nobody's there, but us.

EXT. SARAH'S HOUSE, FRONT DOOR — SAME

The rain pours down on the DOUBLE STROLLER — standing sentinel over the front door.

INT. MCGORVEY HOUSE, UPSTAIRS HALLWAY — NIGHT

MOVE down an UNKNOWN corridor. Stop at the end, outside a closed door. MAY MCGORVEY, 70, small, frail, and fierce, leans in and listens. She reaches up and gently knocks. Nothing. She knocks again.

> MAY
> (gently quiet)
> ...son?

No answer.

> MAY
> ...son?

She turns to go.

> MAY
> (almost to herself)
> ...dream well.

She pads back down the hallway.

INT. MCGORVEY HOUSE, MAY'S ROOM — NIGHT

May lies in bed reading, *THE FIVE PEOPLE YOU MEET IN HEAVEN*. She closes the book, and places it on her night table. She stares up at the ceiling towards the heavens. A change begins to come over her. She grabs the EAST WYNDAM HERALD lying next to her, and quickly sorts through the sections until she finds what she's after.

> VOICE
> May knew it wasn't natural for a grown
> man to be living with his mother, no
> hobbies, no diversions — It was like he
> was still in prison.

She folds the Herald so that it's manageable, grabs a RED FLAIR PEN
from her bedside, and begins circling things in the newspaper.

> VOICE
> What he needed was a girlfriend, and May
> intended to help him find one.

TICK, TICK .....

INT. MCGORVEY HOUSE, LIVING ROOM — MORNING

TICK, TICK, TICK. ANSONIA clocks line every available table, side
table, and shelf, in the room. Shelf space is at a premium though.
Most are adorned with HUMMEL PORCELAIN FIGURINES: little boys in
charming Bavarian garb depicting the gentle innocence of childhood:
*Afternoon Nap, Under an Umbrella, Star Gazer, Newsboy, Playing with
a Train,* and *A Flower for Mother.* Someone is a serious collector.
That someone is —

MAY, who sits in a swivel BARCALOUNGER with a folded NEWSPAPER on
her lap, a PAD and PENCIL in her hands. She stares across the room
to where Ronnie sits sipping coffee from a mug, and reading *Soldier
of Fortune* Magazine.

> MAY
> There are two whole columns of lonely
> women here, and only a handful of men.
> The odds are on our side. Why wouldn't
> one of these women want to meet a nice
> person like you?

> RONNIE
> I'm not a nice person.

> MAY
> You did a bad thing. But that doesn't
> mean you're a bad person.

> RONNIE
> I have a psychosexual disorder.

> MAY
> You're better now. They wouldn't have let
> you out if you weren't.

> RONNIE
> They let me out because they had to.

May looks nervous.

> MAY
> Well, maybe if you found a girlfriend
> closer to your own age, you wouldn't have
> the bad urges so often.

                    RONNIE
          I don't want a girlfriend my own age
          Mommy. I wish I did.

                    MAY
          What're you gonna do when I'm gone? Who's
          gonna take care of you?

Ronnie looks alarmed. He gets up and sits at his mother's feet.

                    RONNIE
          Whatsa matter Mommy? You sick or
          something?

                    MAY
          I'm an old woman. I'm not gonna live
          forever. Who's gonna cook for you? Who's
          gonna wash the dishes?

                    RONNIE
          I can wash the dishes.

                    MAY
          You never washed a dish in your life.

                    RONNIE
          I could if I had to. I'm not a retard.

She reaches out and takes his hand.

                    MAY
          No, you're not... you're a miracle
          Ronnie... we're all miracles. You know
          why? Because as humans, every day we go
          about our business, and all that time we
          know — we *all* know, that the things we
          love, the people we love — at any time it
          can all be taken away... we live knowing
          that, and we keep going anyway. <u>Animals</u>
          don't do that.

A moment.

                    MAY
          Now, I'm not asking you to get married
          Ronnie. I'm just saying put an ad in the
          paper. See what happens.

Ronnie sighs; she's worn him down.

                    RONNIE
          Fine. I'll do it if it'll make you happy.
          But just one date, alright?

May beams. She scribbles something on the pad.

                    MAY
          You have a nice smile. Why don't we start
          with that?

Ronnie seems pleased, but also hungry for more praise.

                              RONNIE
                    What else?

May seems to be at a momentary loss, then —

                              MAY
                    You always eat what I put in front of
                    you. You never complain.

She writes down these things but before she can continue —

                              RONNIE
                    What else.

                              MAY
                         (confident)
                    You're trying to get back in shape. You
                    exercise.

Ronnie beams. May steals a look at her son, then continues the list.

INT. MCGORVEY HOUSE, ENTRY WAY — LATER — MORNING

Ronnie walks his YELLOW SCHWINN ten-speed past the kitchen, and heads
to the front door.

                              MAY (O.C.)
                    Wait right there, young man.

May comes into the hallway from the kitchen.

                              MAY
                    If you're going out for some exercise,
                    you can post this now.

She hands him an envelope. He glances down the address —

The East Wyndam Register — ATTN: PERSONALS DEPT.

                              RONNIE
                 Hmmm.

He opens the front door.

EXT. MCGORVEY HOUSE — MORNING

Ronnie stands framed in the open threshold. The FRONT DOOR behind him
is plastered with LARRY'S FLYERS affixed with DUCT-TAPE. He stares
out toward something as yet unseen, and smiles. He continues to stand
there a moment, and then walks his bike off the porch. He gets on and
rides down the -

DRIVEWAY, across which is spray-painted a singular word — E V I L

INT. SARAH'S HOUSE, ATTIC UTILITY ROOM — DAY

Brad stands nude, facing out the narrow window. A moment later, a
nude Sarah rises up behind him, puts her arms around him, and reaches
around to his crotch.

                         SARAH
                    (breathing hard)
               C'mon. Let's do it again.

                         BRAD
               Okay. Just gimme a second. It's hotter
               than hell up here. What's wrong with the
               laundry room?

                         SARAH
               No mattress. C'mon lie down.

They fall onto a mattress on the floor, surrounded by long forgotten
attic storage. Boxes, and things once belonging to Richard's mother.

                         SARAH
               You're nervous, aren't you?

                         BRAD
               Whatta you mean?

                         SARAH
               The game. Don't worry. You're gonna be
               great tonight.

                         BRAD
               I don't know, I haven't played in ten
               years. It used to be such a big part of
               my life. Then when I stopped, I just
               stopped. I didn't even miss it. But now
               that I'm doing it again... I feel... I
               don't know I —

                         SARAH
                    (cutting him off)
               You feel alive.

There is something about the certainty with which Sarah says this
that runs through Brad like a lightning bolt. He looks into her eyes,
and his face suddenly relaxes.

                         BRAD
               ... yeah.

                         SARAH
               That's good. That's how you're supposed
               to feel.

Brad smiles. They both roll onto their backs, and contemplate this
fact.

                         BRAD
               You're right. It's just been a while.

                         SARAH
                    (to herself)
               Yeah.

They continue to lie there together. Comfortable in silence.

EXT. MCGORVEY HOUSE, DRIVEWAY — DAY

CLOROX BLEACH is splashed onto the graffitied concrete. MAY, on all
fours, scrubs and scrubs.

EXT. EAST WYNDAM BOMBERS' MIDFIELD — NIGHT

The two teams stand facing each other, BULLHORN BOB, in his ELECTRIC
WHEELCHAIR, between them.

> BULLHORN BOB
> (grunts)
> Shake.

No one moves.

> BULLHORN BOB
> (impatient)
> Shake!

The *Auditors* stand stone-faced and utterly silent during the ritual,
like heavyweight boxers trying to intimidate a challenger during
weigh-in.

The *Guardians* refuse to be intimidated. Finally, Brad starts to
extend his hand.

CORRENTI gives him a dirty look. Horrified by his lack of resolve.

But the *Auditor* directly across from BRAD, a MASSIVE BEARDED MAN,
begins to smile, like someone who smells weakness. He extends his
hand to Brad.

As if this is some kind of collective signal, the rest of the
Auditors do likewise.

BULLHORN BOB looks up from his wheelchair at a ceilinged canopy of
clasped hands, like the top of a rainforest.

> BULLHORN BOB
> (raising his bullhorn)
> Toss!

The men step back, and lower their arms.

> BULLHORN BOB
> (to the Auditors)
> Call it!

Somebody grunts, *"heads."* Bob flips a QUARTER high into the air.

It comes down *heads.*

The *Auditor* across from Brad points toward the *Guardians.*

BRAD looks terrified.

CLOSE ON: THE FACE OF A STOPWATCH.

BOB'S RIGHT THUMB hovers over the BUTTON.

ON THE FIELD

THE *GUARDIANS* are set to receive.

The *Auditors'* KICKER raises his hand, and brings it down in a chopping motion.

BOB'S FACE fills with the sadistic expectation of someone watching the beginning of a bloody cock-fight — BOB'S THUMB sends the TIMEPIECE'S SWEEPING HAND into MOTION. TICK, TICK, TICK...

INT. BRAD'S HOUSE, BRAD & KATHY'S BEDROOM — NIGHT

Kathy glances at the clock: 10:07 PM. She looks over at Aaron's cherubic face, asleep on the bed next to her. She settles back onto a pillow pile, grabs the phone, and hits speed-dial.

                    KATHY
          Hi, Mom, I wake you?

SPLIT SCREEN - Meet MARJORIE, Kathy's Park Avenue mother, elegant, well read, and divorced. She's up late trying to finish reading Galway Kinnell's *Black Light*. She reluctantly puts the book down.

                    MARJORIE
          No, dear. Is everything okay?

                    KATHY
          I'm fine.

                    MARJORIE
          You don't sound fine.

                    KATHY
          There's nothing wrong. I just wanted to
          say hi.

                    MARJORIE
          Well hi. So how's my little guy?

                    KATHY
          Great he's sleeping right next to me.
          What a cutie.

                    MARJORIE
              (like clock work)
          So where's Brad?

                    KATHY
          Out.

                    MARJORIE
          I'm surprised the library stays open this
          late.

No she's not.

                    KATHY
          He's not at the library. He's playing
          football with his buddies.

                    MARJORIE
          Football? Honey. Nobody plays football
          this time of night.

                    KATHY
          These idiots do. He comes home with
          scrapes and bruises all over his body.

                    MARJORIE
          Do you remember when your father took up
          golf?

                    KATHY
          He's not like dad.

                    MARJORIE
          Honey, they're all the same.

                    KATHY
          Well, *he's* not.

                    MARJORIE
          You work so hard. I could keep an eye on
          the boys while you're at work, make sure
          they're staying out of trouble. Do you
          want me to come up for a visit?

                    KATHY
               (firm)
          Mom, don't come up here.

                    MARJORIE
          I just worry about you guys. What are you
          going to do if he fails the test again?

                    KATHY
          He's not going to fail.

                    MARJORIE
          That's what you said last time...how're
          you doing for money?

                    KATHY
          Fine.

                    MARJORIE
          I'm gonna send you a little extra this
          month.

                    KATHY
               (losing patience)
          Mom.

                    MARJORIE
               (cheerfully)
          It's no burden. I'm happy to help.

EXT. EAST WYNDAM BOMBERS' STADIUM, GANGBOX, — LATER

BULLHORN BOB inserts a KEY into a PADLOCK, and removes the cover of a
large ELECTRICAL MAIN. He reaches up and kills the stadium lights.

INT. "TALK OF THE TOWN" TAVERN — NIGHT

With the exception of two players, the entire *Guardian* team sits
front and center at a table in the middle of the place. They turn in
unison as Brad & Larry make an entrance through the front door of the
establishment. Larry looks like shit.

                    VOICE
          Although the Guardians lost by 26 points,
          Brad felt oddly exhilarated in the bar
          after the game.

Brad & Larry move across the bar room toward the *Guardians*.

                    VOICE
          ...he could feel a new respect in the way
          the cops looked at him...

PETE OLAFFSON stands, and grabs a couple of chairs for the guys. Brad
& Larry sit. DEWAYNE slaps Brad on the back.

                    DEWAYNE
          Big Brad! Whatcha drinking, buddy?

                    VOICE
          ...he wasn't on probation anymore; he was
          a member of the team.

TOMMY CORRENTI stands and moves behind Brad. He massages Brad's
trapezoids, like an old-time boxing trainer.

                    CORRENTI
          Oh man. You are gonna be one sore puppy
          tomorrow morning.

                    DEWAYNE
          Advil. Advil and ice. Ice and Advil.

                    OLAFFSON
          Don't forget the Ben-Gay.

                    WILLIAMS
          And if all else fails, you can always
          consult our team physician.

WILLIAMS grabs a shot glass from a cork-lined tray in the center of
the table, and offers it to Brad.

                    WILLIAMS
          Dr. Daniels. His friends call him Jack.

Williams pours Brad a shot of Bourbon. Brad raises his glass.

                    BRAD
          To the good Doctor.

He throws back the shot.

                    BRAD
          I feel better already.

The men cheer approvingly, all except Larry, who stares sullenly into his beer.

INT/EXT. LARRY'S VAN — MOVING — LATER

Brad stares over at an uncharacteristically silent Larry, who holds an ice-bag to his eye while driving. Finally -

> LARRY
> I had no business being out on that field tonight. I let you down. I let the whole team down. I'm slow and I'm fat and I let those guys piss all over me.

> BRAD
> Oh, come on. That guy was off-sides the whole night.

A moment.

> LARRY
> Joanie left me. Took the kids and went to her mother's.

> BRAD
> Jesus, Larry. That's a tough break.

> LARRY
> I deserved it. Me and my big mouth. I called her a fucking whore. Right in front of the kids.

> BRAD
> Why did you do that?

> LARRY
> I don't know. I was in a bad mood or something? Now I'm fucked.

Brad watches his friend - worried. He tries changing the subject.

> BRAD
> Hey, you hear about the pervert? He went swimming at the Town Pool.

> LARRY
> What?

Larry whips his head in Brad's direction, turning his attention completely away from the road.

> LARRY
> Who told you that?

> BRAD
> (bragging)
> Nobody. I saw him myself. During the heat wave.

                    LARRY
               (erupts)
     The Town Pool? That place is crawling
     with kids. Sometimes my boys go there.

                    BRAD
               (nervous now)
     It was just that one time. He won't be
     back.
               (reassuring)
     The cops came.

                    LARRY
               (paranoid)
     Any of the guys from the team?

                    BRAD
     ...no.

Larry starts shaking his head and muttering to himself, as if
something were very, very wrong.

Brad looks like he wishes he hadn't brought it up.

Larry STEPS ON THE GAS.

                    BRAD
     Larry, slow down. SLOW DOWN LARRY!

Larry SPINS THE WHEEL HARD to the LEFT, pulling a cop-show U-turn. The
van does an about-face and SPEEDS STRAIGHT TOWARD US.

A HYPERACTIVE DOORBELL RINGS OVER -

INT/EXT. MCGORVEY HOUSE, FRONT DOOR — LATER

May answers the door after the fifth ring. She doesn't seem surprised
to find two men — one of them with a bruised and puffy eye, the other
with a bag of ice pressed against his cheek — standing on her front
stoop at two thirty in the morning.

                    MAY
               (sharp and alert)
     What now?

                    LARRY
     Good evening, Mrs. McGorvey. We were
     wondering if Ronnie was home.

                    MAY
               (snapping)
     You leave him alone.

                    LARRY
     We just want a moment of his time, just a
     little chat.

May turns toward Brad as if he were the one doing the talking. He
looks embarrassed and uncomfortable

                              MAY
                        (firm)
            This is my house. I pay the mortgage, and
            I say who is and isn't welcome.

Larry cups his hands around his mouth.

                              LARRY
                        (shouting)
            Yoo hoo, Ronnie! Get your perverted ass
            down here!

May steps back inside and tries to slam the door, but Larry catches
it with his foot, and kicks it open even wider.

                              MAY
            I'm calling the police.

                              LARRY
            I hear they're well-disposed to child
            molesters.

All the air goes out of the woman. RONNIE himself appears in the
hallway behind her, blinking and bewildered, clad in pajamas.

                              RONNIE
            It's okay, Mommy.

He gently insinuates himself between his mother and the men.

                              RONNIE
            Can I help you gentlemen?

Larry takes an aggressive step toward Ronnie, but May's maternal
instinct kicks in, and she steps in front of her son.

                              MAY
                        (a demand)
            Ronnie, you go on upstairs.

He recedes back into the house.

                              RONNIE
                        (like a three-year-old)
            Alright, Mommy.

Brad grabs Larry's arms and tries to restrain him.

                              BRAD
            Come on, Larry. Let's go home. I think he
            gets the point.

                              LARRY
            You listen to me, you piece of shit. You
            stay the fuck away from the Town Pool,
            you hear me? Or I will personally fix it
            so that you no longer have a dick to show
            anyone, is that clear?

                              MAY
                        (fierce)
            You're a **BULLY!**

May steps forward and gets right into Larry's face. She address the following directly to Brad.

                    MAY
          My Ronnie would never do anything like
                (pointing to Larry)
          He did.

Larry looks scared for the first time.

                    MAY
                (in for the kill)
          That poor child at the mall —
                (with disgust)
          What you did to him.

It's his turn to have the wind knocked out of him. May steps back inside the house, and closes the door with no resistance.

INT. LARRY'S VAN, PARKED — MOMENTS LATER

A worried-looking Brad sits in the passenger seat staring at Larry. For once Larry is silent, and entirely still. He stares down at the steering wheel like a man who has fallen into the deepest possible abyss.

                    BRAD
          Larry?

He doesn't respond.

                    BRAD
          Larry?
                (careful)
          What did she mean by that?

Larry looks up, furious.

                    LARRY
          Oh, don't pretend you don't know about
          me! Everybody knows! *Everybody!*

Larry looks like he may hit Brad.

Brad's hand slips down to the door, ready to jump out if he has to.

                    BRAD
                (careful, but sincere)
          Honest, Larry. I don't know anything. I
          mean I remember hearing something a few
          years ago when we first moved here.
          Something about a shooting at the mall,
          but that's about it. I didn't even know
          you then.

Larry looks convinced. Then embarrassed.

                    LARRY
          I'm sorry...sorry.

Brad just stares at him.

                    BRAD
               (nods)
          ...okay, Larry.

Larry stares down at his hands. Then up to Brad.

                    LARRY
          I still can still see that boy's face,
          staring up at me.

A moment.

                    LARRY
               (by rote)
          Dispatch said there was a shooter loose
          at the mall...It was the end of my shift.
          Ten minutes — ten minutes and it woulda
          been someone else.

Brad watches his friend disappear. All the air is out of him.

                    BRAD
          But it was an accident. You were trying
          to stop the guy, and the boy got caught
          in the crossfire right?

                    LARRY
          No. I panicked. There was no shooter.
          Just the boy. Antoine Harris was his
          name. Big for his age, only thirteen-
          years-old. He was a good kid. Thought it
          was a big joke, waving around an airgun
          at his friend at the *Big 5*. They were
          acting out a scene from some movie they
          liked. Shop girl saw it from across the
          way... called 911.

                    BRAD
          Jesus, Larry — that's terrible.
          But you didn't know. It coulda been real.

                    LARRY
          But it *wasn't*.

Silence.

                    LARRY
          His parents...uh..his parents. I had to —

Larry starts to choke up, and Brad looks away, uncomfortable with
this kind of intimacy.

                    LARRY
          I was diagnosed with post-traumatic
          stress syndrome by three different
          psychiatrists. That's why I retired. I
          couldn't do the job anymore... For a year
          or two Joanie was okay with me hanging
          around the house. But now she thinks I'm
          lazy.

                         BRAD
          Well, why don't you do something else?

                         LARRY
                    (snapping)
          Like what? Drive a fork lift at *Costco*?

                         BRAD
          Maybe you could go back to school.

Larry stares daggers into Brad.

                         LARRY
          I loved my job. I don't want to do
          anything else.

Larry's gaze drifts back to the McGorvey's front porch.

                         LARRY
          You ever think about the term *homeland
          security*? I mean *really* think about it?

INT. EDITING ROOM — DAY

A BOY of 8, TRAVIS, sits on the couch in his living room, his feet
dangle over edge not touching the floor. He stares at his hands.

                         KATHY'S VOICE (O.C.)
          The day you found out that you're father
          had been killed in Iraq. Do you remember
          that day?

The boy looks up from his hands.

                         KATHY'S VOICE (O.C.)
          Can you talk about that? Do you feel
          comfortable talking about that?

The boy nods.

                         TRAVIS
          ...after the men came to tell my mom... I
          cried. But she didn't. She just went into
          her room... grabbed the pillows off the
          bed, and cut the tops off em with a pair
          of scissors... there were feathers all
          over the place.

                         KATHY'S VOICE (O.C.)
                    (gently)
          That must have really frightened you.

                         TRAVIS
          No. She was trying to find the crown.

                         KATHY'S VOICE (O.C.)
          ...the crown?

The boy nods to himself.

                         TRAVIS
          The crown you leave in your pillow when
          you've slept on it for a long time...my
          father...

He looks up at an unseen Kathy.

                         TRAVIS
          ...my father had two crowns.

                         KATHY (O.C.)
          Alright, let's stop there.

Kathy and her editor FRANK, 40s and overweight sit in a small dark
room illuminated by two monitors. Frank looks at Kathy, who seems
someplace else.

                         FRANK
          You hungry?

                         KATHY
          ...no

                         FRANK
          Mind if I get some lunch?

                         KATHY
          No. Go ahead.

Frank leaves the room. Kathy stares at the frozen image of Travis'
face. She reaches for the phone and dials. THE MACHINE PICKS UP.

                         KATHY
          Brad?... Brad?... Are you there?... Pick
          up. I know you're there. It's Aaron's nap
          time
                  (hiding her concern)
          ...alright, guess you're out somewhere. I
          love you both, bye.

She hangs up. Glued to the boy's face staring back at her from
monitor.

INT. SARAH'S HOUSE, ATTIC UTILITY ROOM — SAME

All hills and valleys. The curve of a hip traced by a finger tip. It
moves down the waist and continues to the shoulder. Sarah rolls onto
her back, stares up at the ceiling, and smiles. Brad leans in and
they gently kiss. Lovers who are sated, and comfortable lying in each
other's presence. Sarah reaches up and strokes his face.

The SOUND of WOMEN'S VOICES IN ANIMATED CONVERSATION.

EXT. TOWNHOUSE — MAGIC

Jean, holding a large TUPPERWARE container of brownies, herds a
reluctant Sarah up the stairs of a narrow two-story affair.

                         SARAH
          You know, Jean, I don't think I'm up for
          this.

                    JEAN
        Now, don't be silly. It'll be fun.

The women cross the threshold and into -

INT. TOWNHOUSE, ENTRYWAY — MAGIC

A small foyer, flanked on both walls by large framed posters: The first from Chez Panisse, the other a typical country landscape from Provence.

                    SARAH
           (dubious)
      Really?

                    JEAN
        Don't worry, you're not the only little
        sister here tonight.

                    SARAH
           (relieved)
      Oh. That's good.

Sarah peers into the living room, an airy art-filled space lit only by the early evening sun. Several women chat amiably around a coffee table — ONE OF THE WOMEN turns her head toward the foyer. Sarah's expression tightens, as if in sudden pain.

INT. TOWNHOUSE, LIVINGROOM — NIGHT

CLOSE ON Mary Ann's face. She looks offended.

                  MARY ANN
        Did *anybody* like this book?
        Because I really just hated it.

PULL BACK to reveal the BOOK GROUP, four OLDER WOMEN, plus two LITTLE SISTERS, Sarah and Mary Ann. They sit around a coffee table brimming with wine, cheese, fruit & crackers.

                  MARY ANN
        It's so depressing. She cheats on her
        husband with two different guys, wastes
        all his money, then kills herself with rat
        poison. Do I really need to read this?

The book group is dismayed by this blunt declaration.

LAUREL, a youthful sixty year-old, ventures a response.

                  LAUREL
        Well, there *is* a lot of good descriptive
        writing.

The other ladies nod in vigorous agreement. JOSEPHINE, short and plump, takes the baton.

                  JOSEPHINE
        It's supposed to be depressing. It's a
        tragedy. Madame Bovary's undone by a
        tragic flaw.

Next we hear from BRIDGET, a Gertrude Stein look-a-like.

                    BRIDGET
          What's her flaw?

                    JOSEPHINE
          Blindness. She can't see that the men are
          just using her.

                    JEAN
          She just wants a little romance in her
          life. You can't blame her for that.

                    BRIDGET
          It's about women's choices. Back then a
          woman didn't have a lot of choices. You
          could be a nun or a wife. That's all
          there was.

                    JOSEPHINE
          Or a prostitute.

Mary Ann fixes her gaze pointedly on Sarah.

                    MARY ANN
          She had a choice. She had a choice not to
          cheat on her husband.

                    BRIDGET
          Usually it's the man who cheats. I found
          it refreshing to read about a woman
          reclaiming her sexuality.

                    MARY ANN
          Reclaiming her sexuality? Is that a nice
          way of saying she's a slut?

                    JOSEPHINE
               (miffed)
          Madame Bovary is *not* a slut. She's one of
          the great characters in Western
          literature.

An uncomfortable silence. Then -

                    LAUREL
          I was a little puzzled by the some of
          the sexual references.

She opens her PAPERBACK, annotated with POST-IT TAPE FLAGS.

                    LAUREL
          Like this one. "He abandoned every last
          shred of restraint and consideration. He
          turned her into something compliant,
          something corrupt."

Sarah's fallen into a kind of REVERIE.

INT. SARAH'S ATTIC UTILITY ROOM — DAY

Sarah leans back on the mattress. Brad's head buried between her legs.

INT. TOWNHOUSE, LIVINGROOM — BACK TO SAME

               LAUREL
      Does anyone know what that means?

               MARY ANN
      It means she's a slut.

               LAUREL
      Do you think he's tying her up or
      something?

                BRIDGET
        (sotto)
      Anal sex.

Josephine nods, looking uncomfortable.

               LAUREL
      Did everyone get that but me?

               JEAN
      Let's set that aside for now.
        (glancing at Sarah)
      I'm really eager to hear what our other
      little sister has to say.

Jean raises her voice to get Sarah's attention.

               JEAN
      I'm not sure if you know this, but
      Sarah's got a Ph.D. in English Lit.

Sarah startles to the present, picking up her cue.

               SARAH
      Just a Master's. I never wrote my
      dissertation.

               JEAN
      Well, you still have a lot more *expertise*
      than the rest of us.

Mary Ann rolls her eyes at this. Then levels them at Sarah.

Sarah smiles at Mary Ann, as if the two of them are friends.

               SARAH
      I think I understand your feelings about
      this book. I used to feel the same way
      myself. When I read it in grad school,
      Madame Bovary just seemed like a fool. She
      makes one foolish mistake after another.
      But when I read it this time, I just fell
      in love with her. She's trapped. She can
      either accept a life of misery or struggle
      against it. And she chooses to struggle.

               MARY ANN
      Some struggle. Jump in bed with every guy
      who says hello.

                    SARAH
          She fails in the end. But there's
          something beautiful and even heroic in
          her rebellion. My professors would kill
          me for even thinking this, but in her own
          strange way, Emma Bovary is a feminist.

                    MARY ANN
          Oh, that's nice. So now cheating on your
          husband makes you a feminist?

                    SARAH
          No. It's not the cheating. It's the
          hunger. The hunger for an alternative.
          And the refusal to accept a life of
          unhappiness.

The other ladies beam with approval and fascination.

Mary Ann just shakes her head in disgust.

                    MARY ANN
          Maybe I didn't understand the book. She
          just looked so *pathetic*...

INT. SARAH'S ATTIC UTILITY ROOM — DAY

BRAD stands behind SARAH making love, reaching new heights of
abandon, performing an ECSTATIC DUET of GRUNTS, GASPS, and WHIMPERS.

                    SARAH
                 (breathing hard)
          Is she pretty?

                    BRAD
          Who?

                    SARAH
          Your wife.

INT. BOOK-GROUP TOWNHOUSE — BACK TO SAME

                    MARY ANN
          ...degrading herself for nothing.

INT. SARAH'S ATTIC UTILITY ROOM — ANOTHER DAY

Brad slips Sarah's bra straps off her shoulders.

                    SARAH
          It's a simple question.

                    BRAD
                 (frustrated)
          She's pretty, okay? Do we have to talk
          about this now?

INT. BOOK-GROUP TOWNHOUSE — BACK TO SAME

> MARY ANN
> I mean, did she really think a man like
> that was going to run away with her?

Sarah is beginning to wonder about this herself.

> SARAH
> (uncomfortable now)
> ....possibly.

INT. SARAH'S ATTIC UTILITY ROOM — ANOTHER DAY

After sex, Brad leans back against the wall to catch his breath.
Sarah pokes his chest with her foot.

> SARAH
> How pretty is she?

He stares at her for the longest time. Then —

> BRAD
> (truthfully)
> ...a knockout.

Sarah winces as if she's been struck.

> BRAD
> (patiently)
> Beauty's overrated, Sarah.

INT. SARAH'S BEDROOM — NIGHT

Richard dead to the world. Sarah WIDE AWAKE beside him.

> VOICE
> *Brad* had meant this to be comforting, but
> at three in the morning it had precisely
> the opposite effect. He had a beautiful
> wife, a *knockout*, and she was sleeping
> beside him right now.

MOVE IN on SARAH forcing her profile into the foreground.

> VOICE
> Only someone who took his own beauty for
> granted would have been able to say
> something so stupid, and with a straight
> face.

MOVE PAST HER FACE TOWARD A WALL PAINTING WHICH DISSOLVES INTO —

EXT. BRAD'S FRONT PORCH — DAY

Brad steps out his front door, wearing swim trunks, and hugging a
PICNIC COOLER to his chest.

                    VOICE
          Weekends were difficult for Sarah, forty-
          eight-hour prison stretches separating
          one happy blur of weekdays from the rest.

He lugs it down the steps and stows it in the trunk of a COROLLA. He
glances out toward the street and -

INT. SARAH'S CAR — MORNING

Looking haggard, Sarah ducks down in the driver's seat, trying to see
without being seen.

                    VOICE
          Sarah sometimes let herself be carried
          away by fantasies of a future very
          different from the life she was living
          now. A future without obstacles, in which
          she and Brad were free to love each other
          in broad daylight...

EXT. BRAD'S HOUSE — CONTINUOUS

Aaron comes out next, clutching a PLASTIC BEACH PAIL and SHOVEL, and
heads to the car.

                    VOICE
          ...in which all the mistakes of the past
          were erased, and they had no one to
          answer to but each other.

KATHY emerges, wearing tight shorts and a black bikini top, looking
taller, thinner and more glamorous than Sarah had let herself imagine
in her worst self-loathing insomniac nightmare.

Kathy RAISES HER ARMS and STRETCHES, a vision so lovely it hurts.

INT. SARAH'S CAR — CONTINUOUS

Sarah slinks even lower in the seat, biting her hand to keep from
crying out.

EXT. BRAD'S STREET — CONTINUOUS

The Corolla backs out of the driveway and heads down the street,
passing the apparently empty Volvo.

                    VOICE
          It could happen, she thought. *It had to.*
          Because she wasn't sure she could keep
          living like this for very much longer.

Sarah resurfaces from the floor of the car looking completely
devastated.

EXT. TOWN POOL — DAY

Brad and Sarah back in their usual weekday spot. They eye each other
warily, as if something's changed.

                        BRAD
          You okay?

                        SARAH
          Yeah, fine. How about you?

                        BRAD
          Me? Great. So, uh, how was your weekend?

                        SARAH
          You really want to know? — it sucked. How
          was yours?

                        BRAD
          Terrible.

Surprised, she turns toward Brad.

                        SARAH
          Really?

                        BRAD
          Yeah. Kathy and I went to the beach, but
          all we did was fight the whole time.

Sarah tries to look concerned rather than excited.

                        SARAH
          You did?

                        BRAD
          Yeah. It was are annual argument. About
          taking the bar exam, like our whole life
          depends on it.

                        SARAH
          Just get it over with. You'll feel
          better.

                        BRAD
          Yeah, but it's the whole thing...I gotta
          leave town on Wednesday, take a train —
          it's a two day ordeal...and I'm not even
          gonna pass.

                        SARAH
          You'll do fine.

                        BRAD
          No, I won't. I haven't cracked a book all
          summer.

In spite of themselves, they both laugh.

                        SARAH
          ...I missed you.

                        BRAD
          I missed you too.

A moment.

                          SARAH
          Don't... don't do it.

                          BRAD
          What?

                          SARAH
          Blow it off.

She turns to him suddenly conspiratorial.

                          SARAH
          We should go somewhere, ya know just for
          a night. Richard's out of town till
          Friday, and I'm sure I can get a sitter
          for Lucy.

Brad chews this over, then shakes his head.

                          BRAD
          I can't... do that. I gotta take the
          test.

Sarah tries to look understanding, but her face betrays her.

INT. BRAD'S HOUSE, BATHROOM — MORNING

Brad puts on a clean dress shirt getting ready for a big couple of
days. Aaron sits on the sink watching his father prepare. Brad
reaches over and strokes the boy's mane.

INT. BRAD'S HOUSE, KITCHEN — MORNING

Kathy & Aaron sit at the kitchen table, finishing their breakfast.
Brad has his head buried in a pile of law books - last minute
cramming.

                          KATHY
          Well, I have a good feeling about this.
          I'm gonna buy a bottle of champagne.
          We'll put it in the fridge and open it
          when we get the good news.

                          BRAD
          Don't get your hopes up. We've been down
          this road before.

She smiles at him as though he's a child returning to school after a
brief illness.

                          KATHY
          This time it'll be different. I can feel
          it.

EXT. EAST WYNDAM STATION — MORNING

Kathy's Corolla pulls curb-side, Brad exits the passenger side
holding his briefcase & overnight bag and watches Kathy drive off.

He checks his watch, heads into the station and straight to the
ticket counter.

He shoots a look out the door of the station, then runs back outside just as Sarah's Volvo pulls up. He checks to see if the coast is clear — satisfied he jumps into the front passenger seat and the car takes off.

INT/EXT. SARAH'S VOLVO, MOVING/ROUTE 128 — MORNING

Brad stares out at the scenery.

                    SARAH (O.C.)
          Can you believe it?

Brad glances at Sarah, who looks prettier than we've ever seen her, her eyes bright with adventure, stray ringlets and unruly corkscrews of hair blowing across her face.

Her hand moves lightly over his thigh.

                    SARAH
          It's our first date. A date. Without the
          kids, I mean.

                    BRAD
          How was Lucy? She cry or anything?

                    SARAH
          You kidding? With Jean there? She just
          about shoved me out the door.

Brad glances back at Lucy's empty car seat.

INT. SARAH'S HOUSE, SUN ROOM — DAY

Jean, holding Lucy, tapes colored streamers back & forth across the room, getting ready for their party.

LATER. Lucy watches wide-eyed as Jean opens a tackle box. Step-like shelves emerge, stocked with FELT, GLITTER, GOLD STARS, COLORED CONSTRUCTION PAPER, SEA GLASS, BUTTONS, ROUNDED SCISSORS and PASTE, a cornucopia of crafts supplies.

                    JEAN
          I thought today we could make something
          really beautiful. I've got so many things
          here. We could make a picture frame, or a
          jewelry box, a hat? Whatever you like.

Lucy smiles.

                    LUCY
             (with certainty)
          Something for my Mommy.

                    JEAN
         Okay.

Lucy's hand reaches toward the items, hovering over each one, finally pausing over a small, unfinished, wooden picture frame.

INT. MCGORVEY HOUSE, BATHROOM — DAY

Shaved and showered, clad in beige Dockers and a new collared shirt, Ronnie stands in front of the bathroom mirror. May fusses from behind.

> RONNIE
> Stop it. Just stop it!

> MAY
> Hold on, Ronnie. Just hold on.

With a pair of scissors, she cuts a price tag off the shirt.

> MAY
> (bubbly)
> There. You look handsome. She won't be disappointed.

> RONNIE
> Wait'll she hears about my criminal record.

> MAY
> I don't think you need to get into that just yet. Why don't you stick to small talk?

> RONNIE
> What if someone recognizes me?

> MAY
> That's highly unlikely. I made the dinner reservation at a restaurant over in Haverhill.

THE SOUND OF CHILDREN'S LAUGHTER

INT. STEAK HOUSE — NIGHT

RONNIE gazes across the place at a nearby booth, where A FAMILY with TWO YOUNG CHILDREN, a BOY & GIRL, ages 9 and 10, start on their dessert. The children laugh as their FATHER and MOTHER engage them in some kind of game.

Ronnie, with great difficulty, pulls his attention away from them, and takes the last bite of his food. He looks across the table at SHEILA, who stares down at her plate. She hasn't touched a bite.

> RONNIE
> Sheila?
> (louder)
> Sheila?

This produces the desired effect. She looks straight at Ronnie for the first time.

> SHEILA
> Yes?

                    RONNIE
          What's the matter? Something wrong with
          the food?

                    SHEILA
          ...no.

                    RONNIE
          Back at the house you mentioned you were
          on medication.

Sheila nods compliantly.

                    RONNIE
          What kind?

                    SHEILA
          Oh, all kinds. Mostly psychotropic.

                    RONNIE
          So you had some kind of a breakdown?

Sheila nods.

                    RONNIE
          When?

                    SHEILA
          My junior year in college.

                    RONNIE
          You were that young?

Shelia nods. Grateful for his interest and concern.

                    RONNIE
          What happened?

                    SHEILA
          ...I'm not really sure.

                    RONNIE
          Nervous breakdowns don't just come outta
          nowhere. Something musta caused it.

Sheila sits in front of her untouched meal, concentrating hard, as if
responding to a therapist.

                    SHEILA
          I guess. But I was fine when I left for
          college. Maybe it was the stress of being
          on my own. Maybe it was a chemical
          imbalance in my brain. Every psychiatrist
          I go to has a different opinion. This one
          guy, Dr. Farris, said I must have been
          sexually abused as a child. When I told
          him I wasn't, he just said I was
          repressing the memory.

Uncomfortable, Ronnie changes direction.

                         RONNIE
               Right. So what happened after that? You
               drop out of school?

                         SHELIA
               Not right away. My mother sent me to the
               campus counselling center. And they
               wanted the problem fixed. Like I could
               just snap my fingers and everything would
               be okay again.

                         RONNIE
                    (sincere)
               Oh yeah. I know all about that.

                         SHEILA
               You do?

Ronnie leans forward.

                         RONNIE
               Yes. I do.

Sheila smiles.

                         SHEILA
                    (on a roll now)
               Either that or leave school, get married,
               and have lots of kids like my sisters.
               But I can't take care of kids. I can't
               even take care of myself half the time.
               Besides, who's gonna marry me?

Ronnie takes her in.

                         RONNIE
               You're not so bad.

Startled by Ronnie's complimentary tone, Sheila smiles, shyly.

                         SHEILA
               ...what?

                         RONNIE
                    (shy)
               You're not...you're not so bad.

Sheila beams.

                         SHEILA
               I haven't had a real boyfriend in six
               years... not since my second breakdown.
               Something happened to me on a Greyhound
               Bus. I ended up in —

The WAITER arrives, interrupting her.

                         WAITER
                    (to Sheila)
               Do you want me to wrap that up?

> SHEILA
> (still staring at Ronnie)
> What? Oh, no thank you.

> RONNIE
> (to waiter)
> Yes. Wrap it up, please. I'll take it home.

> WAITER
> You folks gonna want dessert?

> RONNIE
> What do you say Shelia? You want to share
> something sweet?

Shelia just stares at Ronnie. Smitten.

EXT/INT. SHEILA'S BUICK, MOVING — NIGHT

Ronnie & Sheila ride in silence.

> RONNIE
> Let's make a little stop. Take the next left.

She suppresses a smile, enchanted by his take-charge attitude.

INT/EXT. SHEILA'S BUICK, WALKER STREET PARK — NIGHT

The Buick is parked on an empty street with its HEADLIGHTS still on.

> RONNIE
> Turn off the lights.

Sheila switches them off.

Sheila faces straight ahead, so does Ronnie.

The date seems to have had a positive effect on Sheila, or maybe the
medication's wearing off. Her voice sounds livelier, a little less
spacey.

> SHEILA
> I had a nice time tonight.

Ronnie doesn't reply.

> SHEILA
> The last guy I went out with, you know
> what he did? He ditched me. Got up to go
> to the men's room, and never came back.
> Stuck me with the check. Never said
> goodbye, never called to apologize.

Still nothing from Ronnie.

> SHEILA
> He wasn't my type anyway. He was this
> super normal guy, a big-shot CPA. He
> didn't want to be dating some psycho.

A smile plays at the corners of her mouth.

                       SHEILA
        But you seem like a nice person.

She turns slowly, as if volunteering for a kiss. It is only then that she sees what he is up to.

His right hand begins moving up and down on his lap, and his breathing rapidly increases.

Shelia watches from the corner of her eye. She sort of hums to herself, like a child on a ride that they are frightened of, and hope will be over soon.

Ronnie looks up at her, his face fierce.

                       RONNIE
        You better not tell on me.

Shelia continues to hum.

                       RONNIE
            (louder)
        You hear me?!

She nods — but begins to cry.

                       RONNIE
        You better not tell, or I'll fuckin' get
        you.

Ronnie stares at her as he huff and puffs. His eyes stray slightly to the left, and just past her.

She turns away from him suddenly, and it is only then that the true focus of Ronnie's attention is visible out the driver's window —

THE PLAYGROUND

EXT. MCGORVEY HOUSE — NIGHT

Sheila's car pulls up at the curb. Ronnie gets out, holding his DOGGIE BAG from the restaurant. Without a word her car speeds away.

INT. MCGORVEY HOUSE, MAY'S ROOM — SAME

May stands at her bedroom window watching her son cross to the front door. The look on her face, tragically hopeful.

EXT. EAST WYNDAM STATION — MAGIC

The five-o-clock pulls into the station and commuters disembark, Brad among them. He crosses the platform and makes his way over to the family car —

Kathy sits waiting in the driver seat. Aaron, securely fastened in his car seat, oblivious to his mother's hopes and expectations. Brad arrives and gets in.

Kathy makes a quick study of her husband's demeanor.

                    KATHY
          So?

                    BRAD
          What?

                    KATHY
                 (laughing)
          The test, dummy. How'd it go?

                    BRAD
          ...alright.

                    KATHY
          I was worried. You never called home last
          night.

                    BRAD
          Guess, I could really use that cell phone.

Kathy is caught off-guard by this response. She decides to ignore it.

INT/EXT. SARAH'S HOUSE, SUNROOM — MAGIC

Sarah grabs her overnight bag from the car and heads toward the
sunroom. The place is transformed: STREAMERS, DRAWINGS on glass
panes, and a HOME MADE SIGN on butcher paper running the width
of the room: UPPER CASE letters written by Jean, and pictures of
people with CIRCLE BODIES, AND LINES OUT OF THEIR HEADS by Lucy -

The sign reads: *WELCOME HOME MOMMY*

Sarah eyes the place warily, then turns from the room and heads
outdoors. She rounds the side of the house, looking to make a more
comfortable entrance through the kitchen door.

SARAH'S HOUSE, KITCHEN — MAGIC

Sarah enters to find Jean sitting at the table, knitting and
listening to NPR.

                    JEAN
          Look who's back.

                    SARAH
          Thanks, Jean. You're a lifesaver.

                    JEAN
          So how's your old roommate?

                    SARAH
          Oh great, great. Thanks for doing this on
          such short notice.

Sarah reaches into her bag, and pulls out her wallet.

                    SARAH
          I want to give you something for your
          time.

The woman looks surprised, and somewhat insulted.

                              JEAN
                 That's not necessary.

Sarah pulls some bills out.

                              SARAH
                 No, really. I insist.

Jean's face wears the look of someone who has just discovered what a
person she thought was a friend, really thinks of her.

                              JEAN
                         (sharply)
                 Please don't.

                              SARAH
                 ...okay.

Jean begins gathering up her knitting and her craft box.

                              SARAH
                 Any calls?

                              JEAN
                 No, it's been very quiet.

Jean heads to the kitchen door.

                              JEAN
                 She's asleep on your bed. We had a very
                 busy day.

                              SARAH
                         (uncomfortable)
                 Well, that's great. Thanks again.

Jean heads out the door.

                              SARAH
                 Jean, is everything okay?

Jean turns around and looks at Sarah. She is about to honestly answer
her question, but decides to bite her tongue instead.

                              JEAN
                 ...yes. She's a wonderful child.

Without another word she makes for home.

INT. SARAH'S HOUSE, BATHROOM EN SUITE — MAGIC

Sarah enjoys a hot shower, mentally reliving her afternoon, while
erasing any traces of it at the same time.

SARAH'S BEDROOM — SAME

Lucy lies asleep on her parent's bed, her tiny arms curled around a
square object. After a moment the child wakes. Her ears perk to the
sound of running water, coming from the bathroom.

STILLS

                              LUCY
                          (muttering)
          Mommy?

SARAH'S BATHROOM — SAME

Sarah shuts off the water, squeezes her hair, steps out of the
shower, wraps her towel into a turban, and gazes into the mirror,
trying to find that sweet spot, that perfect angle.

A tiny knock on the bathroom door.

                              LUCY (O.C.)
          Mommy?

Sarah sighs, and closes her eyes, fantasy interrupted.

                              SARAH
          ...yes?

                              LUCY (O.C.)
          Are you coming?

SARAH'S BEDROOM — SAME

Lucy stands on the other side of the bathroom door. In her hands, her
project for the afternoon.

                              LUCY
          I have something.

                              SARAH (O.C.)
          What?

                              LUCY
          I have something for you.

Silence, then -

                              SARAH (O.C.)
          Give me a minute here, okay?

Lucy stands there a moment, then walks away - depositing her mother's
gift onto the bed on her way out of the room.

The gift is something of rare value: Buttons adorning a frame, within
which rests a photo of Lucy herself.

INT. BRAD'S HOUSE, BEDROOM — NIGHT

Kathy and Brad lie back-to-back. Neither one of them can sleep.
Finally —

                              KATHY
          Brad?...Brad?

                              BRAD
          Hmmm?

                    KATHY
         Aaron was telling me today all about his
         new friend, Lucy.

Brad, still turned away, grimaces.

                    KATHY
         She sounds like a sweet little girl...

Brad looks momentarily relieved. Then –

                    KATHY
         ...What's the *mother* like?

A moment.

                    BRAD
         ...Uh, nice enough, I guess...
                    (yawning)
         I can't even remember her name.

                    KATHY
         Isn't it *Sarah*?

Silence.

                    BRAD
         ...Sarah?

                    KATHY
         Yeah. *Sarah*? From the pool? She has a
         little girl named Lucy?

                    BRAD
         Oh, Lucy's mom. I forgot, that's right,
         her name's Sarah.

Kathy decides to push further.

                    KATHY
         I think it would be nice for Aaron if we
         all had dinner together.

Brad looks horrified.

                    BRAD
         ... okay.

INT. BRAD'S HOUSE, LIVING ROOM – NIGHT

Nodding off, Aaron and Lucy lie side by side, surrounded by a warm
yellow canopy of light, and the drone of their parents conversation.

TWO TINY PAIRS of FEET protrude from a tent fashioned from polished
miniature SAW HORSES draped with YELLOW SILK. Grown-ups in the middle-
distance.

INT. BRAD'S HOUSE, DINING ROOM — NIGHT — CONTINUOUS

Kathy sits next to Sarah, both sipping their wine. They've made themselves comfortable with each other while secretly sizing each other up at the same time.

Brad listens to Richard — who's mid-story in an oft-told tale about his product consulting business.

>   BRAD
>   So, you're in adverting?

>   RICHARD
>   No. That's a common mistake. I'm in
>   *branding*. And that's really very
>   different.

>   SARAH
>   Richard's pretty high up in the company.

Kathy smiles at Sarah's seeming support of Richard. She shoots a look to Brad as if to say, "isn't it sweet how proud she is of this dolt?"

Brad smiles back at his wife.

This is not lost on Sarah, and she begins eating at a rapid pace.

>   RICHARD
>   Yeah, yeah, yeah. Like the other day
>   these guys come to me, and they want to
>   start a chain of Chinese restaurants.

He pause for dramatic effect.

>   RICHARD
>   And not one of them is *Chinese!*

Everyone at the table is sort of waiting for the punch-line, which never arrives.

Brad and Kathy force polite laughter. Sarah looks miserable. Fortunately, Brad tries to pick up the thread.

>   BRAD
>   Well, where were they from?

>   RICHARD
>   They're a bunch of fat cats from
>   Tennessee. But they think they can create
>   a chain of restaurants authentic enough
>   to fool the average American boob.

More forced laughter from Brad & Kathy. Sarah wishes Richard would just shut up. She turns to Kathy, and tries to change the subject.

>   SARAH
>   (re: dinner)
>   This is delicious.

>   KATHY
>   Isn't it?

She looks across the table at Brad, and smiles.

                    KATHY
          Brad's a *fantastic* cook.

Sarah is nearly at the end of her rope, and uncertain how much longer
she can endure this very strange dynamic.

                    RICHARD
          So, have you seen these flyers with the
          guy's face plastered all over the
          village? Lots of sturm and drang in our
          quiet little town, eh?

                    BRAD
          It's crazy.

                    RICHARD
          What I want to know is why they let a
          creep like that out of prison.

                    SARAH
          Some of the people going after him are
          just as crazy.

                    KATHY
          What do you mean?

                    SARAH
          Well, just today I heard that some nut's
          been spray-painting the poor guy's house,
          lighting fires on his porch, and God
          knows what else.

Brad shrinks.

                    KATHY
          Do they know who's doing it?

                    SARAH
          They think it's some ex-cop.

Kathy glances at Brad.

                    SARAH
          You know, that guy who killed the kid at
          the mall.

                    BRAD
               (almost too fast)
          I don't think it's him.

                    KATHY
          You're biased.
               (to Sarah)
          Brad is friends with the guy. They're
          both on that *Committee of Concerned
          Parents.*

Sarah stares at Brad, perplexed.

                         SARAH
          I didn't know you were on that.

                         BRAD
                       (nervous)
          I play on his football team. And he asked
          me to distribute some flyers.

                         SARAH
                       (wounded)
          He's on your team? You never told me that.

Kathy looks startled. It's odd to hear such a possessive tone coming
out of another woman's mouth. She studies the dynamics of the table.
Every gesture, and every word, now viewed through a microscope.

                         RICHARD
          You know what's weird? I've never even
          seen this McGorvey guy.

                         SARAH
          We did.

                         RICHARD
          No, we didn't.

                         SARAH
                       (reclaiming her position)
          Not you. Me and Brad. That day at the
          pool, remember?

Brad is unable to mask his discomfort with this question.

                         BRAD
                       (to Sarah's question)
          Oh yeah, I forgot.

Kathy stares at Brad.

                         VOICE
          Sexual tension is an elusive thing, but
          Kathy had pretty good radar for it. It
          was like someone had turned a knob a
          hair to the right...

Kathy's view shifts to the RIGHT - To now include SARAH IN THE FRAME
WITH BRAD for the first time in the scene.

                         VOICE
          ...and the radio station clicked in so
          loud and clear it almost knocked her
          over. Once she became aware of the
          connection between them, it seemed
          impossible that she'd missed it before.
          On a hunch...

Kathy steals a look toward her own hand as it -

Inches toward her FORK.

                         VOICE
          Kathy dropped her fork...

Her hand "accidentally" knocks the FORK to the FLOOR. It falls end-over-end in SLOW MOTION.

She slips under the table to retrieve the utensil.

> VOICE
> ...in the hopes that while retrieving it she would catch Sarah and Brad playing footsie.

Kathy stares at the forest of legs beneath the table. No footsie of any kind is in progress.

> VOICE
> But she was mistaken.

Kathy looks frozen, like a deer in the headlights, not sure what to do next. She makes no move to join the others.

> BRAD (O.C.)
> Kathy? Are you okay?

Kathy's tries not to hyperventilate.

She stares dumbstruck at SARAH'S ridiculously PAINTED TOES.

> KATHY
> Yeah...just a sec.

INT. BRAD'S HOUSE, BATHROOM — NIGHT

Brad stares into the mirror with a big forced grin on his face. The image is absurd until his hand appears with a TOOTHBRUSH and he begins his nightly regime.

> VOICE
> Brad had convinced himself the dinner party had gone well, that he and Sarah had managed to put Kathy's suspicions to rest, at least temporarily.

INT. BRAD'S HOUSE, BEDROOM — NIGHT

He emerges from the bathroom and heads over to join Kathy, who is already in bed.

> VOICE
> She certainly hadn't accused him of anything, or behaved in a way that made him think she'd noticed anything untoward.

Brad pulls the covers up and glances at Kathy. She smiles.

> KATHY
> I'm *really* glad they came over.

Brad smiles back, confident that his deception has been a success. He leans over, kisses her on the cheek, then reaches up and kills the light.

BLACK

                        VOICE
            Two days later, however...

EXT. BRAD & KATHY'S HOUSE — DAY

A CHAUFFEUR opens the door of a TOWN CAR, and Kathy's mother emerges
from the back. She scans the house with hungry anticipation.

                        VOICE
            ...his mother-in-law showed up for a
            "surprise visit" of ominously
            indeterminate length. And from that
            moment on, she accompanied Brad and
            Aaron everywhere.

EXT. WALKER STREET PLAYGROUND — DAY

                        VOICE
            To the playground...

Brad pushes Aaron & Bear on the swings. He glances toward the picnic
table formerly occupied by the busybodies, only to be met by the
suspicious stare of his mother-in-law.

EXT. SHAW'S SUPERMARKET, CHECKOUT — DAY

                        VOICE
            To the supermarket...

Aaron sits in a SHOPPING CART; Brad and Marjorie stand in a long
checkout line, not speaking a word to one another.

Brad's eyes drift toward the magazine rack and land innocently on a
bikini-clad model on the cover of *Fitness.*

As he turns his attention back to the line, he becomes aware of
Marjorie's sternly disapproving face.

EXT. TOWN POOL — DAY

                        VOICE
            ...and to the town pool.

Brad & Aaron are in their usual spot, with the addition of Marjorie.

Brad cranes his neck, pretending to reach for something in his bag,
stealing a melancholy glance at SARAH, who's sitting under a nearby
tree.

                        VOICE
            The worst of it was the pool.

Her LARGE SUNGLASSES make it impossible to tell if she's even
noticed.

                        VOICE
            Nevertheless...

INT. BRAD'S HOUSE, LIVING ROOM — NIGHT

                    VOICE
          ...after threatening all week to go the
          football game...

Kathy and Marjorie sit next to each other on the couch, staring
across the room, like two people safely behind Plexiglas, watching a
venomous snake at the reptile house.

                    VOICE
          ... Brad's mother-in-law decided against
          it at the last minute.

Across the room, Brad bends over to tie his sneaker.

                    BRAD
          You sure?

He tries to keep the pleasure out of his voice.

                    BRAD
          You're welcome to come.

                    MARJORIE
          I'd like to, but I'm a little tired. You
          and Aaron sure kept me hopping this
          afternoon.

                    KATHY
          Looks like you're on your own tonight.

Marjorie pats Kathy affectionately on the leg.

                    MARJORIE
          Besides, I need to spend a little time
          with my daughter. We've hardly said two
          words since I got here.

The familiar SOUND of LARRY'S HORN interrupts her.

Brad leaps up and heads for the door.

                    BRAD
          That's my ride.

                    KATHY
          What time will you be home?

                    BRAD
          Dunno. But pretty late, though.

                    MARJORIE
              (forced smile)
          Be careful. And stay out of trouble.

BRASS FANFARE & KETTLE DRUMS - AN INTRO WORTHY OF NFL FILMS

EXT. EAST WYNDAM BOMBERS' STADIUM — NIGHT

<u>A PASSENGER TRAIN SPEEDS BY ON AN ELEVATED TRANSOM</u>. THE VIEW SHIFTS
AWAY FROM THE TRACKS & toward a darkened FOOTBALL STADIUM. Through
the lens of NFL FILMS, we experience the following —

CLOSE ON AN AMERICAN FLAG wafting in the summer air.

> VOICE
> Winds whisper of high hopes, victory is
> in the skies.

SLOW ZOOM OUT from the flag high above the stadium, as banks of PAR
LIGHTS burst on, one panel at a time, illuminating -

The empty bleachers.

> VOICE
> One joins with many on Summer's green
> field.

...on the field, the GUARDIANS are lined up for the opening kick-off.
Their opponents, the CONTROLLERS, a bunch of spandex-clad, twenty-
something gym heads, are set to receive.

> VOICE
> At 0-5, the Guardians were the basement
> dwellers of the Tri-County Touch Football
> Night League.

BART WILLIAMS, with his hand in the air, looks to the sideline, where —

BULLHORN BOB, stopwatch in hand, blows his whistle.

WILLIAMS boots the BALL, and the GUARDIANS charge downfield.

> VOICE
> The Controllers, a team of young hotshots
> from the financial district, were 4-1,
> with an explosive offense that regularly
> racked up 40 to 50 points a game. But
> from the opening kick-off...

The CONTROLLERS' speedy RETURN MAN is gang-tackled by FOUR ferocious
GUARDIANS.

> VOICE
> ...this ragtag group of law enforcement
> officers decided to crunch their own
> numbers.

DEWAYNE SAVAGES NUMBER 39.

CORRENTI CLOTHESLINES NUMBER 12.

BRAD SUBMARINES NUMBER 28.

WILLIAMS AND OLAFFSON SANDWICH NUMBER 39 AGAIN.

> VOICE
> But the Controllers scored first, after
> recovering a Bart Williams fumble deep in
> Guardians territory near the end of the
> second quarter.

Controllers' NUMBER 39 struts in the end zone, while BART clutches his head in dismay.

> VOICE
> The Guardians evened things up early in
> the second half...

BRAD completes a slant pass to DEWAYNE.

BART rushes up the middle, struggling for six yards.

> VOICE
> ... moving methodically downfield...

BRAD pitches the ball to DEWAYNE, who turns the corner with CORRENTI and LARRY blocking.

> VOICE
> ...on an 80-yard touchdown drive.

BRAD throws a short pass to DEWAYNE for the score.

> VOICE
> The Controllers regained the lead with a
> fourth quarter field goal.

The ball tumbles end over end through the goalposts.

BULLHORN BOB raises his hands, signalling, "It's good."

> VOICE
> With less than a minute to go, trailing
> by three, the Guardians faced the
> extinction of their hopes. It was their
> last chance, fourth and five on their
> own thirty-five.

CLOSE ON BRAD'S HANDS, opening like a clamshell against LARRY'S ASS as he takes the snap.

BRAD bootlegs right, looking first for RITCHIE MURPHY, his short man. Covered.

Ditto on BART, his middle receiver.

BRAD cocks the ball, ready to throw to —

DEWAYNE, his last and best chance, only to watch him slip and fall as he makes his cut.

BRAD loops back to avoid the pass rush. He looks up to see open field ahead. He tucks the ball and runs. Fifteen, twenty, twenty five yards, the field pitching toward him with each pounding stride.

THE CONTROLLERS begin to gain on him. Out of nowhere DEWAYNE pulls up beside him to run interference, but THE CONTROLLERS NUMBER 39 trips up DEWAYNE, leaving BRAD exposed to THE CONTROLLERS speed demon NUMBER 23. He's only inches away from the tackle when suddenly LARRY, screaming like a banshee, flies between the two men and flattens THE CONTROLLER.

THE CONTROLLERS, NUMBER 9 catches up to BRAD as he crosses the fifteen yard-line. BRAD slams on the brakes so drastically and unexpectedly that his pursuer simply goes zooming past him with a desolate cry of protest, stumbling out of bounds and leaving BRAD with a clear path to the end zone. He spins on his heels and jogs backwards into the end zone, the ball raised triumphantly overhead. He spikes the ball, his arms stretch wide, his chest heaving.

BRAD searches the STANDS for a witness to his glorious moment. To his surprise, he sees —

SARAH in the top row of the BLEACHERS - she's seen it all. The music crescendoes to a finale as their eyes meet.

The NFL FILM sequence morphs into our previous reality

EXT. EAST WYNDAM BOMBERS' STADIUM, BLEACHERS — LATER

Larry appears to be the only player remaining. He zips up his GYM BAG, and then looks out across the field, scanning it for his friend.

                    LARRY
              (calling out)
          Brad?

No answer.

Finally, he spots TWO SHADOWY FIGURES embracing in the END-ZONE.

Larry hesitates, then walks back onto the field, and makes his way toward Brad and Sarah. He stops near the ten yard-line.

                    LARRY
          Brad?

Brad looks up, pissed.

                    BRAD
          What do you want?

                    LARRY
          All the guys are waiting for us at the
          bar. Are you comin'?

                    BRAD
          Why don't you go ahead. I'll catch up
          later.

                    LARRY
          You're gonna come, right? We need to
          celebrate.

                    BRAD
          Yeah, yeah. I'll be right there.

                    LARRY
                 (desperate)
          You promise?

                    BRAD
          Jesus, Larry. I just told you.

                    LARRY
          Well...you got a ride?

                    BRAD
          YEAH.

Larry turns to go.

                    LARRY
          Ok. I'll have a cold one waiting for you.

Larry stomps off.

INT. "TALK OF THE TOWN" TAVERN — NIGHT

The place is empty save for Larry, who sits at the bar, utterly alone.
TWO BEERS, and TWO SHOTS lined in front of him waiting for Brad's
arrival. Larry stares at the glasses with heartbreaking expectation.
KEN, the bartender, stands directly across from Larry — looking every
inch the man who is about to kick Larry's ass.

                    KEN
          Larry? Larry!?

Larry finally looks up.

                    KEN
          You need to go home.

                    LARRY
          Just give me five more minutes he
          promised he was coming.

                    KEN
          I don't care what he promised. I need to
          lock up. Now get your butt out of here.

Larry doesn't move.

                    KEN
             NOW!

EAST WYNDAM BOMBERS' STADIUM, END ZONE — NIGHT

Brad and Sarah lie on their backs together looking up at the night
sky. Still high from his triumph, Brad bubbles with an animated
enthusiasm.

                    BRAD
          When I looked up and saw you — it was
          just. Wow. Wow. Thank God you came. I
          don't want to go home. I want to stay
          right here forever.

                          BRAD (CONT)
          For the first time in my life I feel like
          I can do anything. Like anything's
          possible. You know?

Sarah rolls onto her side to look at him. Her eyes are wet and puffy,
her voice husky with emotion.

                          SARAH
          What are we doing here?

                          BRAD
          Whatta you mean?

                          SARAH
          It's not real, Brad. It's wrong, and it's
          weird. How long are we going to sneak
          around together? How long can that last?

                          BRAD
          No. Don't say that.

Brad looks like his high is very likely on the way to a terrible crash.

                          BRAD
          I want you to listen to me, Sarah.
          As long as I know we're going to have
          this, as long as —

                          SARAH
                    (cutting him off)
          Have what? What is *this*? Look if that
          dinner party at your house was any
          indication...you seem pretty happy with
          your wife. I mean you have this perfect
          life and I don't want to be the one
          that...

Something comes over him. He can't lose this ground. Not tonight. He
immediately kicks into high gear. He leans in to her.

                          BRAD
          Run away with me.

                          SARAH
          What? You...you don't mean that.

                          BRAD
          You *believe* in me.

His new confidence excites and frightens her.

                          BRAD
          C'mon. We'll go away — figure this thing
          out... It's not _weird_. The kids are
          comfortable with each other. I know
          there's more to it than that, but let's
          do this. Please. Please, Sarah.

He kisses her deeply. Then pulls back slowly.

Sarah's face reacts with the force of someone who has just won the
Lotto but has no idea where to redeem the ticket.

                    SARAH
                 (breathless)
        ...Okay.
                 (giggling)
        Yes. Yes.

EXT. "TALK OF THE TOWN" TAVERN, PARKING LOT — LATER

Larry sits on the curb outside the entrance of the place, muttering.
His head buried in his lap, like a jilted lover.

                    LARRY
        Brad.... Fuckin' Brad. I'm so sick of
        hearing about that guy... OOOH Brad made
        the Fuckin' touchdown.... Yeah, you know
        why he didn't have the balls to show up
        here tonight? Because I made the fuckin'
        block... that's why he can't even look at
        me. He's embarrassed to even see me.

Larry has worked himself into quite a lather. Then —

                    LARRY
                 (furious)
        I hate everyone in this fuckin' town.

THE SOUND OF TIRES SCREECHING ON PAVEMENT

                    LARRY (O.C.)
                 (into a bullhorn)
        WAKE UP!

INT. MCGORVEY HOUSE, MAY'S BEDROOM — NIGHT

May lies in bed, her eyes open as if from a bad dream.

                    LARRY (O.C.)
        WAKE UP! WAKE UP WOODWARD COURT!

May sits up in bed.

                    MAY
                 (as if to God)
        Okay, I'm awake.

                    LARRY (O.C.)
        OPEN YOUR EYES! GET YOUR GOD DAMN HEADS
        OUT OF THE SAND!

                    MAY
                 (confused)
        My heads? My God damn heads?

She stands too quickly, and has to sit back down to recover. She
takes a breath. Then slowly makes her way to the window.

                    LARRY (O.C.)
        DON'T YOU PEOPLE LOVE YOUR CHILDREN?
        DON'T YOU WANT TO PROTECT THEM FROM EVIL?

May pulls up the SHADE and looks down to see Larry standing in front
of her house.

                              LARRY
               WOODWARD COURT! THERE'S A PERVERT IN YOUR
               MIDST. THERE'S A GOD DAMN PERVERT IN YOUR
               MIDST.

INT. MCGORVEY HOUSE, UPSTAIRS HALLWAY — SAME

Larry's voice continues to emanate through the place.

The hallway light switches on. May crosses out of her bedroom,
throwing on a robe, while heading to the stairs.

Ronnie's head peaks out of his room.

                              MAY
               It's okay, Ronnie. Just stay inside.

May hurries downstairs.

EXT. WOODWARD CT. — SAME

HOUSE LIGHTS up and down the street domino on. As Larry's rant continues.

EXT. MCGORVEY HOUSE, FRONT STOOP — SAME

The door opens on a very angry May, dressed in a NIGHTGOWN & ROBE.

                              MAY
               You dirty son—of—a—bitch! Get off my lawn!

In a frenzy, she runs toward Larry in her bare feet.

                              MAY
               Who the hell do you think you are? Mr.
               High and Mighty?

Larry ignores her.

                              LARRY
                        (through bullhorn)
               NO PERVERTS AT THE TOWN POOL! NO PERVERTS
               AT THE TOWN POOL!

                              MAY
                        (shouting)
               You think you're God? Far from it.

Larry inadvertently addresses her through the bullhorn.

                              LARRY
               I KNOW I'M NOT GOD. I NEVER SAID I WAS.

                              MAY
               You're the murderer. You killed the boy.

Larry lowers the bullhorn.

                              LARRY
               I didn't murder anyone. Now why don't you
               go back inside and put some clothes on.

                        MAY
            You shot him through the neck.
            I read it in the paper.

To his amazement, May lunges for the bullhorn, and tries to rip it
out of his hands. She has no chance against his strength. He raises
it into the air, and her along with it.

                        MAY
                    (angry)
            Give me that. Just give it to me.

                        BIG GUY'S VOICE (O.C.)
            Hey, Mister. You need to go home.

Larry glances over his shoulder, and sees two men standing by the
curb - a BIG GUY in lightweight pajamas, and a LITTLE GUY dressed in
a robe.

                        LITTLE GUY
            The police are coming.

                        BIG GUY
            You're scaring my kids. I wish you'd cut
            it out.

                        LARRY
                    (grunting)
            Your kids need to be frightened.
            They live across the street from a
            pervert.

A SIREN BLARES IN THE DISTANCE

Larry's ears prick up at the threat, he looks down the street and
then makes one last tug on the bullhorn. The momentum sends May
tumbling backward onto her lawn. This goes unnoticed by Larry as he
moves toward the sidewalk to see which direction the squad car will
arrive.

The Big Guy and Little Guy run over to where May has fallen.

                        LITTLE GUY
            Oh, My God! Mrs. McGorvey are you okay?

She's flat on her back, and unconscious.

                        BIG GUY
            May!? *May*!? I think we better call and
            ambulance.
                    (shouting)
            Karen! Call an ambulance right now!

                        KAREN (O.C.)
            I'm doing it.

Larry finally sees what has happened, and tentatively makes his way
over. He stares at May's twitching limbs and hears an AWFUL GURGLING
NOISE coming from somewhere deep in her throat. Her eyes are WIDE
OPEN, staring straight into his. Her lips are moving, but there
aren't any words coming out. He looks scared.

LARRY
Oh, Fuck. This is all I need.

EXT. MCGORVEY HOUSE, FRONT YARD — LATER

GUMBALL LIGHT Rakes everything. People in nearby houses gawk from their porches. Other neighbors make their way down the street to get a better look at the scene.

MAY, attached to O2 and an IV DRIP, lies supine on a GURNEY as she is loaded into a waiting ambulance by two EMT's.

LARRY sits in the back of a POLICE CRUISER watching it all.

A POLICE OFFICER leads RONNIE away from his mother's side, and back toward the front of the house. Ronnie turns his back on the cop. At this moment he is only interested in looking at one man —

LARRY — locked in the backseat of the squad car.

Ronnie's gaze is filled with an intensity we have never seen.

Larry, sees it too, and is the first to look away.

EXT. TAXICAB, EAST WYNDAM PRESBYTERIAN HOSPITAL — NIGHT

A cab pulls up to the curb. Ronnie gets out of the car, holding a WOMAN'S TRAVEL CASE, and heads toward the hospital entrance.

INT. ICU, WAITING ROOM — NIGHT

A TELEVISION mounted from the ceiling drones *Bloomberg*.

Other than a TEENAGE GIRL, reading Time Magazine, Ronnie is alone. A hand appears in front of him, holding a CUP OF COFFEE. He looks up in surprise to see -

A 30 year-old PUERTO RICAN WOMAN extending the beverage.

PUERTO RICAN WOMAN
Cafe con leche?

He nods, gratefully taking the cup from her hand. She sits down beside him and drinks from her own cup.

She opens her wallet and leans over to him, displaying its contents:

A Sears portrait of an older Puerto Rican woman.

PUERTO RICAN WOMAN
Madre.

Ronnie pats his pockets, and realizes he has no photo of May to share. He nods to the woman.

RONNIE
Me too. She's resting now.

INT. ICU, MAY'S ROOM — SAME

May lies in a hospital bed, attached to a ventilator, catheter, EKG diodes, and drip. A monitor SOUNDS its steady metronomic beep, as A NURSE'S HANDS steady an ENVELOPE that MAY is struggling to address:

"RONNIE"

INT. EAST WYNDAM POLICE STATION — SAME

A HAND, attached to the HASH MARKED SLEEVE of a POLICEMAN'S SHIRT, passes a MAN'S BELT, a PACK OF CHEWING GUM, and a WEDDING BAND across a recess on the underside of a Plexiglas walled counter. On the other side of the divider, a PAIR OF HANDS attached to a familiar SWEAT SHIRT receive the above.

On a PRISONER RELEASE FORM, a signature is made on a line above a typed name — *Larry Hedges*.

A WALL MOUNTED SECURITY MONITOR memorializes the exchange.

EXT. POLICE IMPOUND YARD — LATER

The street is empty, except for Larry, who glances around in all directions, as he makes his way over to a chain-length-fence, and rests his hands against it.

Out of nowhere A BARKING GERMAN SHEPARD leaps spread-eagle onto the fence and tries to bite Larry.

Larry, safely on the other side, jumps back, startled.

A LARGE MAN with a pot belly emerges from the impound office and pulls the dog back.

> LARGE MAN
> Get down — knock it off!

He grabs a chain that is permanently fastened to the side of the building and attaches it to the animal's collar. Then opens the chain-length-fence. The dog continues to bark.

Larry backs away, putting as much distance between himself and the Shepard as he can. Headlights smack Larry in the face as his van emerges from the back recesses of the lot, and pulls up to the fence.

Larry clocks the dog as he steps forward to retrieve his van.

The animal gives a constant low growl, not taking his eyes off Larry for a second.

Larry throws the van into gear, and takes off.

INT. LARRY'S VAN — NIGHT

He drives as if in a trance. Larry looks worriedly down at his right hand, which shakes uncontrollably. He tries to steady it by gripping the wheel, as if his life depended upon it.

INT. ICU WAITING ROOM — NIGHT

Ronnie, asleep in a chair, is alone in the room now. The TV continues to drone in the background.

A NURSE arrives at his side — she takes a seat beside Ronnie and, placing her hand on his shoulder, gently wakes him.

>   NURSE
>   Mr. McGorvey? Mr. McGorvey?

Ronnie stirs.

>   NURSE
>   I'm afraid we have some bad news.

Ronnie just stares at her.

INT. ICU STAFF COUNSELOR'S OFFICE — NIGHT

A windowless office with fluorescent lighting. Day or night — the place remains the same. An ICU COUNSELOR is midway through a speech he's given too many times. By degree, his bedside manner only slightly more sensitive than a veteran police officer reading a perp their Miranda rights.

>   COUNSELOR
>   Do you have a mortuary to make the
>   arrangements for you?

Silence.

>   COUNSELOR
>   It's not a problem. The hospital has a
>   list I can provide you with. Now here's
>   what's going to happen. Your mother's
>   body will remain in her bed for up to
>   three hours. Three hours is typical, but
>   if there is a request for more time,
>   depending on our occupancy, it's usually
>   not a problem. If there's anyone you'd
>   like to call — family, friends, they're
>   welcome to full bedside visitation
>   privileges before the body is taken
>   downstairs to be prepped for transport.
>   Do you have any questions that come to
>   mind?

Ronnie is silent.

>   COUNSELOR
>   Anything we can help you with?

Ronnie finally looks up.

>   RONNIE
>   ...no.

>   COUNSELOR
>   Okay. I'd like to remind you to take all
>   of your mother's personal belongings with
>   you before leaving the hospital today.

                        COUNSELOR (CONT)
         And all I need from you now is to sign
         this release-of-remains form.

He slides a clipboard across the desk.

EXT. HOSPITAL, PARKING LOT — FOLLOWING AFTERNOON

A dazed Ronnie leaves the hospital, clutching May's travel case. He
heads down the sidewalk, but stops suddenly when he sees —

The same cab that dropped him off the night before, waiting at the
curb. Ronnie heads over and gets into the back seat. The car pulls
away.

As it leaves the hospital parking lot it passes —

LARRY, sitting in his van at the other end of the parking lot — watching.

INT. MCGORVEY HOUSE, ENTRY WAY — LATE AFTERNOON

The door opens and closes to RONNIE'S FEET. They make their way
inside, and over to A PAIR of MAY'S SHOES, that sit patiently waiting
for her return.

INT. MCGORVEY HOUSE, MAY'S BEDROOM — LATE AFTERNOON

Ronnie's hands unpack May's travel case. He removes each item, and
gently lays them onto the bed: A compact, a toothbrush, moisturizing
creme, and a hairbrush. He is about to close the lid, when he spots
something on the bottom of the case, <u>AN ENVELOPE with a single word
roughly scrawled across its front</u> - *"Ronnie."*

INT. MCGORVEY HOUSE, KITCHEN — NIGHT

The kitchen light flicks on. Ronnie stands in the doorway, the
unopened envelope in his hand, taking stock of the mess he's made in
the past few days — UNWASHED DISHES piled up in the sink, yesterday's
HALF-EATEN DINNER still sitting on the table, right next to an
OVERFLOWING ASHTRAY.

A *PLAY-TEX* RUBBER GLOVE is tugged over a hand.

The faucet runs, filling a pot with sudsy water.

A determined Ronnie reaches for a sponge & gets down to work.

LATER

The gloves come off, and are tossed in the sink. The kitchen looks
clean.

Ronnie crosses over to the kitchen table and sits.

He stares at the UNOPENED ENVELOPE, now resting in the fruit basket.
He tentatively picks it up, and slowly turns it over in his hands.
How long should he wait to have this conversation with his mother?

He waits, but a moment, and then opens it.

A single line of script, *"Please be a good boy."*

His face begins to contort, as if he's in real pain. He drops the
piece of paper and flees the kitchen.

LIVING ROOM

He flies into the room, talking to himself, while he moves straight
to the many shelves full of HUMMEL FIGURINES. He stares at a myriad
of innocent faces. The little boys & girls in halcyon settings seem
to be mocking him. It is the hour, and suddenly all of the clocks
begin to strike. So does Ronnie. With a frightening intensity —
smashing, throwing, and destroying the figurines, the clocks — all of
it. He displays an energy and determination we have never seen.

INT. BRAD'S HOUSE, HALLWAY — NIGHT

Brad makes his way along the upstairs hallway, stopping outside the
doorway of —

AARON'S ROOM

Brad stands there a moment staring at his, jester-cap clad, son
asleep on his bed.

After a moment, Brad kneels down and shakes the boy awake.

                    BRAD
               (whispers)
          Aaron?

Aaron nods. And sits up a little. Brad takes a deep breath, studying
his son, who gazes back at him with trusting eyes.

                    BRAD
          Aaron?

                    AARON
               (sleepy)
          Yes, daddy?

                    BRAD
               (almost pleading)
          Could you take off your hat for me? Just
          for a second?

To Brad's surprise, Aaron does as he's told.

                    AARON
          Are you mad at me, daddy?

                    BRAD
          No, No, No. I just want you to know that
          I love you very much, and I would never
          do anything to hurt you. Okay?

                    AARON
          ...okay.

Brad leans over and kisses Aaron on the cheek.

                    BRAD
          You can go back to sleep now.

INT. BRAD'S HOUSE, BEDROOM — LATER

CLOSE ON a piece of paper being slipped into an envelope. It rises up to BRAD'S LIPS, and he licks the flap. <u>The front is addressed with a single word</u> - "*Kathy*."

His eyes stray to Kathy's bedside table on which rests a framed picture of husband & wife. Kathy standing in front of Brad — protective.

HALLWAY

Marjorie and Kathy busy themselves with after-dinner clean-up. In the hallway behind them, Brad passes unnoticed on his way to the front door, carrying a SMALL GYM BAG.

He opens the door, glances over his shoulder toward the kitchen, and leaves the house.

INT. SARAH'S HOUSE, LIVING ROOM — SAME

Sarah rounds the bottom of the stairs to find Lucy, in front of the television, watching *Charlie Rose*.

She crosses to Lucy, kneels down, and picks her up.

                    SARAH
          Lucy, come on. Let's go.

EXT. SARAH'S HOUSE — NIGHT

Sarah emerges with the child on her hip, her free hand struggling with the overnight bag and a *Barbie* backpack. She barrels toward her Volvo, opens the back door and is immediately faced with the impossibility of Lucy's car seat.

                    LUCY
          I will not get in the car seat!

Sarah struggles to load her in. Lucy goes completely stiff and straight making this an impossibility.

                    SARAH
          Yes, you will. You will get in the car
          seat.

                    LUCY
          No. I will not.

                    SARAH
                 (pleading)
          Please!?

                                        CUT TO:

THE OPPOSITE BACK PASSENGER DOOR OPENS

Sarah tries to appear calm.

                         SARAH
          Alright, you don't have to get into the
          car seat. You can just lie here.

She lays Lucy onto the back seat. Lucy allows this.

                         SARAH
          No, actually...

She puts the child down on the floor.

                         SARAH
          ...get on the floor. Now just stay
          on the floor. Stay on the floor
          and hide. Or mommy will get
          arrested. Okay?

Sarah shuts the door.

INT. MCGORVEY HOUSE, KITCHEN - NIGHT

Looking wild-eyed and muttering angrily to himself, Ronnie rummages
through a CUTLERY DRAWER until he finds what he's looking for. He
draws his finger along the blade of a BUTCHER KNIFE, testing its
sharpness.

EXT. WALKER STREET PLAYGROUND — NIGHT

Sarah, carrying Lucy, arrives at the playground, entering through the
front gate. Sarah turns and closes the latch with a *clank*.

                         LUCY
          Mommy. I want to go home?

                         SARAH
                      (impatient)
          In a minute. As soon as Brad gets here.

INT/EXT. LARRY'S VAN, MCGORVEY HOUSE — NIGHT

Larry's parked outside Ronnie's house, staring at the front door.

THE SOUND OF A DOORBELL RINGING

INT. MCGORVEY HOUSE, FRONT HALL — MOMENTS LATER

The entry way is unoccupied. No one moves to answer the door. The
ringing stops. We hear the SOUND of knocking, and the door slowly
opens to reveal Larry. He looks nervous, unsure how to proceed
without the obstacle of a gatekeeper.

                         LARRY
          Ronnie?

EXT. MAIN STREET — NIGHT

Brad, carrying his gym bag, walks past the darkened businesses in the
town center. He looks like a robot, or a man heading to the gallows.
Finally he picks up the pace to his normal gate — breaks into a trot,
and then a full out sprint.

EXT. WALKER STREET PLAYGROUND — SAME

Sarah pushes Lucy on the swing. She steals a look at her watch, and
then glances toward the front gate. She turns back around and
continues pushing the swing. Her ears perk up at the sound of RAPIDLY
APPROACHING FOOTSTEPS she smiles. The gate clanks open. She smiles
and turns toward the sound. But instead of finding Brad —

It's RONNIE.

His hands are buried beneath his shirt, and he is moaning. His
hunched-over figure makes his way past her, and over to the swingset
at the opposite end of the park.

                    SARAH
          Oh, my God.

Almost unconsciously, she continues to push Lucy. The metronomic
rhythm some sort of odd comfort. She keeps her eyes trained on this
man, and then steals an expectant look back toward —

THE ENTRANCE OF THE PLAYGROUND.

EXT. MUNICIPAL LIBRARY — SAME

Brad sprints down the street past the library. But at precisely this
moment "G" comes flying through the air on his skateboard, and sails
right across his path. Brad comes to a complete stop. His eyes follow
the boy.

                    "G" (O.C.)
          Hey, dude. What's your hurry?

As if in a trance, Brad walks straight up to the skateboarders, who
are gathered around a steep concrete stairway. He has never been this
close to them. Brad stands next to "G", who watches one of his
minions fly off the staircase. The boy turns to him, extending his
board.

                    "G"
          Why don't you take a run.

                    ANOTHER SKATER
          Give it a shot, see what happens.

                    BRAD
          You guys are crazy.
               (pointing to the stairway)
          I can't do *that*.

                    "G"
          It's not about *that*.

He speaks to Brad as if this is the most important piece of wisdom
one person could impart to another.

                    "G"
          It's about skating.

                                        CUT TO:

EXT. MUNICIPAL LIBRARY — MOMENTS LATER

Brad stands on the board, poised at beginning of a long run of
concrete. He kicks forward gaining speed. The skateboarders urge him
on with shouts, whoops, and cries of encouragement. He will need it.
His approach to the stairway is coming up fast. It must be right.
Here it is. He launches off the stairway, catching an unbelievable
amount of air.

EXT. WALKER STREET PLAYGROUND — SAME

Sarah, trying to ignore Ronnie's presence, glances over her shoulder
expecting Brad's arrival.

The SOUND of Ronnie sobbing is something she can no longer ignore.
She turns to see —

Him hunched over on his swing, crying uncontrollably.

She pauses just a moment, and then abandons Lucy's swing, and makes
her way over toward the other end of the park. Stopping half-way
between the two structures.

She wears a look of uncertainty on her face as she takes a couple of
hesitant steps in his direction.

                    SARAH
          ... do you need help?

He looks up at her in shock, and then nods.

                    RONNIE
              (through tears)
          ...she's gone.

He can hardly get the words out.

                    RONNIE
          ...she's ...gone.

Sarah doesn't know who *"she"* is, even so, she offers what little solace
she can.

                    SARAH
              (gently)
          ...who? ...who's gone?

                    RONNIE
          ... mommy.

                    SARAH
          I'm... I'm sorry.

                    RONNIE
          She loved me.

A moment.

                    RONNIE
          She's the only one.

He drops his head back down, and continues to sob. What he says from this point on is to himself. For him, Sarah no longer exists.

> RONNIE
> Mommy died... mommy died...

Sarah is at a complete loss. She stands dumbstruck for a moment.

The SOUND of the ENTRANCE GATE clanking shut, turns her around, expecting to find Brad.

Instead she finds Lucy's empty swing, swaying back-and-forth.

Sarah panics.

> SARAH
> Lucy?!

Nothing.

> SARAH
> LUCY!!!

Nothing.

The child is nowhere in sight. Sarah scans the tiny playground. The child has disappeared. Sarah sprints away from Ronnie, and begins searching the shadows.

> SARAH
> (screaming now)
> *LUCY!!!!!*

NOTHING

Sarah sprints toward the entrance, and emerges onto —

THE STREET — She looks up and down in both directions. Her face primal, as is her cry.

> SARAH
> *LUCY!!!!!*

A moment of terror that feels like an eternity.

Finally, about a hundred yards down the sidewalk she sees —

LUCY — The child stands at the base of a street light staring up at the lamp, as if hypnotized.

INSECTS flutter in groups, propelling themselves against the vapor.

The child is utterly absorbed.

Sarah's face relaxes. Though it wears the confusion of her sudden outburst and momentary sense of loss.

> SARAH
> Lucy!

Sarah runs to Lucy, scoops her into her arms, and heads to her —

CAR

Almost hyperventilating now.

>   SARAH
>   (angry)
>   Get in the car-seat. Get in the car-seat.

The child does not fight her.

Sarah's sense of urgency verges on panic. She attempts to strap Lucy into the seat, but her shaking hands make a mess of it. Finally she just gives up. Sarah lurches forward and begins to sob uncontrollably into her child's lap.

Lucy looks down at her mother, concerned.

She lifts up her tiny hand and places it on top of Sarah's head — gently stroking it, back and forth.

>   LUCY
>   It's okay, mommy. It's okay.

Lucy continues to caress Sarah's head, and this seems to calm her.

Sarah raises her head up, and looks at her daughter. Her eyes unwavering, transfixed by the child's face, which greets her with unconditional trust. The two suspended together. Nothing else exists.

Lucy stares at her mother curiously.

And it is in this moment that something essential in Sarah completely transforms.

>   SARAH
>   ... oh, Lucy.

She leans forward and embraces her daughter.

>   SARAH
>   I'm sorry... I'm so sorry.

She kisses her daughter's nose, forehead, and cheek.

>   SARAH
>   (whispers)
>   Would you like to go home?

The child nods.

>   SARAH
>   Okay, let's go.

Sarah gets to her feet, closes the back door, and climbs into the front.

EXT. WALKER PARK, RATHBUN AVENUE — NIGHT

Her car pulls away from the park, where, for a split second it
crosses paths with an AMBULANCE heading the opposite direction.
Sarah slows to a safe distance before continuing on her way.

EXT. MUNICIPAL LIBRARY — NIGHT

DeWayne, looking very official, towers over us dressed in a police
uniform. He crouches slowly, his face full of concern.

> DEWAYNE
>
> Brad?

Brad lies flat on his back.

> DEWAYNE
>
> Brad? Can you hear me?

His eyes flutter open.

> DEWAYNE
>
> Don't move, the ambulance is on its way.

He stares up at DeWayne, as if suddenly waking from a dream.

> BRAD
> (groggy)
>
> Jesus, what happened to me?

> DEWAYNE
>
> I don't know, but these kids say you've
> been out cold for the last five minutes.

"G" appears next to DeWayne.

> "G"
>
> Man, you almost had it.

Another boarder joins "G" and DeWayne.

> ANOTHER BOARDER
>
> Dude, you were awesome.

> STILL ANOTHER BOARDER
>
> Man that shit was knarly.

A small smile of satisfaction forms on Brad's face.

> DEWAYNE
>
> Alright back-up. Back-up. Give him some
> room.
> (to Brad)
> Just hold still. Hold still. Everything
> is going to be alright.

EXT/INT. MUNICIPAL LIBRARY, AMBULANCE — NIGHT

Strapped onto a GURNEY, Brad is lifted into the ambulance. The
AMBULANCE ATTENDANT is about to shut the door when "G" interrupts.

"G"
            Hey, bro. This fell out of your pocket.

He extends the envelope addressed to *"Kathy."*

Brad frowns.

                    BRAD
              (waving him off)
        Thanks, I don't need it anymore.

Brad raises his head, making eye contact with DeWayne.

                    BRAD
        DeWayne? Could you call my wife?

                    DEWAYNE
        You got it buddy.

EXT. WALKER STREET PLAYGROUND - NIGHT

From a distance we see Ronnie sitting alone on his swing, still
hunched forward with his hands in his lap, moaning. Slowly we make up
the distance, moving toward him — The SOUND of gravel under moving
feet — Someone is coming.

As we arrive at his back, the crunch of gravel STOPS. Still lost in
his own private hell, Ronnie is oblivious. A large male hand reaches
out and comes to rest on his shoulder.

                    MALE VOICE (O.C.)
        I'm so sorry Ronnie...I really am.

Ronnie's head jolts up. Suddenly present. His face scared, but also
angry. He is looking at —

LARRY

                    LARRY
        I never wanted anything like this to
        happen.

Ronnie just stares at him.

Ashamed, Larry averts his eyes, and stares at the ground.

And he sees something from this proximity that Sarah completely missed
from her vantage point: beneath the seat of Ronnie's swing, <u>drops of
blood trickle to the sand below</u>.

Larry's eyes go wide. He looks up to Ronnie.

                    LARRY
              (scared)
        ... are you...are you okay?

Ronnie smiles.

He stands up and takes a couple of steps away from Larry. He turns to
face him, and drops his pants.

From behind it is apparent he has wrapped his lower extremities in rolls and rolls of cotton gauze — like a paper towel, the white texture rapidly absorbing red.

Larry stares at Ronnie's crotch. Horrified.

>   RONNIE
>   ... I'm... I'm gonna be good now.

Ronnie's legs go rubbery, and he begins to collapse.

Before he hits the deck, Larry catches Ronnie in his arms, lifts him off the ground, and quickly carries him to the —

PARKING LOT

THE SIDE DOOR of the van opens, and Larry carefully lays Ronnie down in back and covers him with a blanket. Larry, now covered in blood, looks down at Ronnie worried.

>   LARRY
>   Hold on Ronnie. I'm not gonna let
>   anything happen to you. You hold on!

He closes the door, and runs around to the driver's side, jumps in, starts the van, pulls a portable GUMBALL light from under the dash and places it onto the roof.

>   VOICE
>   In his wildest dreams, Larry would have
>   never imagined he'd once again be in this
>   position, where precious minutes count.

Larry's van screeches out and tears down the road, driving like there's no tomorrow.

INT. LARRY'S VAN, EAST WYNDAM ROAD - MOVING FAST

RED LIGHT rakes the van interior, and the road ahead.

>   VOICE
>   Tonight he could save a life.

Larry turns in his seat, and screams encouragement to Ronnie in back. Words we cannot hear.

>   VOICE
>   He knew Ronnie had done some bad things
>   in the past — but so had Larry.

EXT. PRESBYTERIAN HOSPITAL, AMBULATORY ENTRANCE — NIGHT

TWO NURSES, and a YOUNG DOCTOR rush forward through automatic doors, and are immediately bathed in red GUMBALL light.

>   VOICE
>   You couldn't change the past...

The GURNEY is pulled out the back of the AMBULANCE, as KATHY rushes past MEDICAL TECHNICIANS to reach BRAD.

INT. SARAH'S HOUSE, LUCY'S BEDROOM - NIGHT

On her side next to a sleeping Lucy, Sarah reaches up and kills the bedside lamp. She remains in the tiny bed with her child.

> VOICE
> ... but the future could be a different story...

EXT. SARAH'S HOUSE, ROOF LINE — NIGHT

Rise with the wind up over roof-tops and tree-tops — All of East Wyndam laid out like a wood-cut in monochromatic relief.

> VOICE
> ... and it had to start somewhere.

A gust kicks up, the trees begin to sing, their branches dance. The distant sound of metal on metal, *ping, ping, ping.*

The view begins to slide back to where we started, looking straight down at the playground, now empty and quiet, save for the chain of a single swing that stubbornly beats its tune into the structure.

BLACK

— THE END —

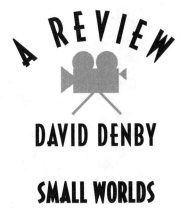

A REVIEW

DAVID DENBY

SMALL WORLDS

Sarah Pierce (Kate Winslet), the thirtyish heroine of Todd Field's extraordinary new movie, *Little Children,* dropped out of graduate school to marry an older man—a business consultant—and moved into a neo-Colonial house near Boston that he inherited from his mother. Some years have gone by, and the marriage is not in the best shape: Sarah's husband communes on the Internet with a friendly person known as Slutty Kay, and Sarah, unwilling to hire any help, feels imprisoned by their three-year-old daughter, whom she (rather negligently) looks after by herself. Sarah is the latest version of the baffled Americans that Betty Friedan wrote about forty years ago in *The Feminine Mystique*—the women supposedly living the American dream. What's particularly embittering in this case is that Sarah knew all about the trap and still stepped into it. Her face pale with disgust, she sits in a tiny suburban playground with three other young mothers who ruthlessly put down anyone who's even slightly different from themselves. These three witches—the only element of caricature in the movie—live on a rigidly controlled schedule. But there's an unaccountable element in their lives: Brad (Patrick Wilson), the good-looking, strongly built young man who makes them all flutter when he shows up at the playground with his little boy. Brad is married to a beautiful filmmaker (Jennifer Connelly) who works for PBS, leaving him at home to take care of the baby and to study for the state bar exam, which he has failed twice. A former golden-boy college jock stranded in adulthood, Brad is decent, not too bright, irresistibly attractive—a man designed for adultery. As the children take their daily nap, Sarah and Brad run to an

DAVID DENBY is a film critic for *The New Yorker*. This review appeared in the October 16, 2006, issue.

empty corner of her house. If they leave town together, where will the kids fit in?

There's an element of garden-variety suspense in *Little Children,* but sex and possible home-wrecking are only part of what the movie is about. *Little Children* is based on a best-selling 2004 novel by Tom Perrotta, who worked on the adaptation with Todd Field. Together, the men have preserved Perrotta's tone, which fluctuates between slightly satirical, even mischievous, irony and the most generous sympathy. Perrotta and Field make you see how their characters are weak or screwed up without allowing you to despise them. Moral realists, they know the world does not yield easily to desire. *Little Children* is a sharply intelligent and affecting view of suburban blues—a much bigger canvas than Field's previous movie, *In the Bedroom* (2001), which was about a placid middle-aged couple thrown into turmoil when their son takes up with an older woman separated from a violent man. Field has grown in ambition, but he still works on an intimate scale. He surrounds his characters with an intense stillness, and then slowly introduces the ungovernable into their lives.

Handsome Brad, it turns out, is not the only disturber of the peace. A convicted sex offender, Ronnie (Jackie Earle Haley), a polite, childlike fellow, has been released from prison and is living in the neighborhood with his mother. For parents who have moved to the suburbs to protect their children, Ronnie's presence is an unbearable outrage. Everyone is obsessed with him, especially a troubled ex-cop (Noah Emmerich), who runs around putting up pictures of Ronnie and forming committees to guard against him. After a while, one realizes that Perrotta and Field may be creating a metaphor of life under terrorism. It's not that Ronnie isn't a genuine threat, but he causes people to lose all sense. At the least, the filmmakers are hinting that both men and women are projecting their sexual frustrations and fears onto a pervert. What fuses Ronnie's story and the rest of the movie is the charged suggestion that outright perversion and ordinary unhappiness (sexual indifference, adultery, porn obsession, semi-psychotic rage) belong on the same spectrum of recognizable behavior. Almost everyone in town has a secret, or at least an itch.

Field works with such fluid grace and perception that the movie goes right to the top of the suburban-anguish genre. The picture is not as aggressively designed or as witty as *American Beauty;* nor is it as malicious as Todd Solondz's *Happiness.* It's smarter, tougher, closer to the common life. Field captures, for instance, the way the daily routines of child care—getting a kid into a car seat or a hat, putting him down for a nap—have to be accommodated within the furious passions of adultery. The picture moves swiftly and surely; the separate shots that evoke the town are fitted together with uncanny precision, and Field neatly pulls off a big set piece that another director might have ruined with overemphasis. When Ronnie jumps into the town pool on a very hot day, the parents scream for their children and haul them out of the water, leaving Ronnie, in a mask, alone under the surface. As the police expel the invader, the children riotously jump back in, and the mass hysteria, followed by mass relief, is both sinister and funny—an interruption of summer pleasure that intentionally leaves our sympathy split between the alarmed parents and the sad outcast.

The sexual awakening of a disappointed wife may seem like an old movie turn, but when has it been done with such candor? At the beginning of the movie, Kate Winslet's hair looks dead, and she hides her body in denim overalls. Her Sarah is a slightly clumsy woman who has lost her confidence. When she falls in love with Brad, the transformation comes slowly and painfully: at first, a nervous gesture, a smile that turns anxious, and then a golden aureole of beauty, a body in movement. The sex scenes are brief, naked, heated, startling. But Winslet never quite loses the awkwardness and uncertainty that will always be Sarah's signature. Brad is not a type, either.

Patrick Wilson, a stage actor who appeared in the movie version of *Phantom of the Opera,* has a slightly puzzled air: his Brad is pleased by the attention of women, but he doesn't think much of himself, and Wilson, as a performer, seems quite without vanity. Looking at teen-age boys flying through the air on skateboards, Brad falls into a rapt silence; his longing for lost youth is so defenseless that it's impossible to dislike him, however irresolute he is as an adult. At first, Sarah and Brad seem prematurely defeated. Yet the filmmakers hold out the possibility of new life stirring under the domestic halter and the intellectual sloth. Adults may not be happier than overgrown children, but at least they have a chance of finding out who they are.

CAST AND CREW CREDITS

New Line Cinema Presents
A Bona Fide
Standard Film Company Production
A Film by
Todd Field

LITTLE CHILDREN

Kate Winslet   Jennifer Connelly   Patrick Wilson   Jackie Earle Haley   Noah Emmerich   Gregg Edelman
Phyllis Somerville   Raymond J. Barry   Jane Adams   Ty Simpkins   Sadie Goldstein   Helen Carey
Sarah Buxton   Mary B. McCann   Trini Alvarado   Marsha Dietlein Bennett   Will Lyman

Directed by Todd Field	Executive Producers Patrick Palmer, Toby Emmerich Kent Alterman	Costume Designer Melissa Economy
Screenplay by Todd Field & Tom Perrotta	Cinematographer Antonio Calvache	Music by Thomas Newman
Based on the novel by Tom Perrotta	Production Designer David Gropman	Production Sound Edward Tise
Produced by Albert Berger & Ron Yerxa Todd Field	Film Editor Leo Trombetta A.C.E.	Casting by Todd Thaler Belinda Monte Stegemann

Associate Producers
Michele Weiss, Leon Vitali

CAST

Sarah Pierce . . . . Kate Winslet
Brad Adamson . . . . Patrick Wilson
Kathy Adamson . . . . . Jennifer Connelly
Richard Pierce . . . . Gregg Edelman
Lucy Pierce . . . . Sadie Goldstein
Aaron Adamson . . . . Ty Simpkins
Larry Hedges . . . . Noah Emmerich
Ronnie J. McGorvey . . . Jackie Earle Haley
May McGorvey . . . . . Phyllis Somerville
The Voice . . . . Will Lyman
Jean . . . . Helen Carey
Marjorie . . . . Catherine Wolf
Mary Ann . . . . Mary B. McCann
Theresa . . . . Trini Alvarado
Cheryl . . . . . . Marsha Dietlein Bennett
Sheila . . . . Jane Adams
Bullhorn Bob . . . . . . Raymond J. Barry
Slutty Kay . . . . Sarah Buxton
Troy . . . . Thomas Greaney
Isabella . . . . Anna Audia
Courtney . . . . Celestial Hakim
Christian . . . . Hunter Reid

Tony Correnti . . . . . . Chadwick Brown
Dewayne Rogers . . . . . Phil McGlaston
Bart Williams . . . . . . Bruce Kirkpatrick
Richie Murphy . . . . Adam Mucci
Pete Olaffson . . . . Chance Kelly
Laurel . . . . Rebecca Schull
Josephine . . . . Crystal Field
Bridget . . . . Lola Pashalinski
"G" . . . . Walker Ryan
Skateboarder 2 . . . . David Cole
Skateboarder 3 . . . . Weston Elrod
Richard's Secretary . . . . Erica Berg
Frank . . . . Leo Trombetta
Steak House Waiter
. . . . Christopher Nicholas Smith
Large Man . . . . Adam Sietz
Small Man . . . . Tom Perrotta
Cabbie . . . . Stan Carp
Kind Woman in Hospital . . . Sandra Berrios
ICU Counselor . . . . Ivar Brogger
ICU Nurse . . . . Myra Turley
ICU Loved One . . . . Alida P. Field
Tow Yard Attendant . . . . David Rowdon

Boy in Kathy's Documentary . . . Paul Mott
EMT . . . . Margaret Pace
Concerned Mom at Pool #1 . . Beatrice Rigaud
Concerned Mom at Pool #2 . . . Mary Goggin
Concerned Mom at Pool #3 . . . . Jillian Lindig
1st Policeman at Pool . . . . William Harvey
2nd Policeman at Pool . . . . Casper Andreas
Lifeguard . . . . Matt Garifo
Snack Girl . . . . Brooke Fazio
Wading Pool Mom . . . . . Monica Dobson
Bartender . . . . Ken Tirado
Children at Steakhouse . . . . Carlie LaPorta
                              Cody Rubenstein
Ted from Richard's Office . . . Joe C. Guest
Ray from Next Door . . . . . Bruce Gross
Auditor Team Captain . . . . Patrick Larkin
Police Officer at McGorvey's . . Michael Diesel

Channel 5 News Segment
Reporter . . . . Jennifer Rainville
Off-screen Anchor . . Gary Anthony Ramsay
Concerned Parent #1 . . Patricia A. Gangemi
Concerned Parent #2 . . . Cynthia L. Wiese
Concerned Parent #3 . . . . . Loren Wiese
Concerned Parent #4 . . . Clare F. Mitchell

Oddly Familiar Man . . . . . . Leon Vitali

Slutty Kay Fan Club Members
. . . . Conrad Angel Corral
                        Darrell E. Geer
                        Gil Ira Hayes
                        Mark A. Pierce
                        Marshall Lefcourt
Background Football Players . . John Begley
                                Mike Ganim
Skateboarders . . . . Travis Koestler
                              Daniel Falla
                              Luis Tolentino
                        Tugman Tookmanlian
Stunt Coordinators
. . . . . . Doug Crosby (Football sequence)
    Erik Martin (Skateboard sequence)

Stunt Doubles
Brad Stunt Double (Skateboard)
. . . . Jamie Balling
Brad Stunt Double (Football)
. . . . David Shumbris
Larry Stunt Double . . . . . Kevin Cassidy

Stunts
Igor Zinoviev   Jeremy Sample
Earle Masciulli   Curtis Lyons
Mario D'Leon   Rocco Forgione

Stunts (continued)
John Cenatiempo   Jared Burke
Tim Lajcik   Valdimar Johannsson

CREW
Unit Production Managers
. . . . Raymond Quinlan
                        Patrick Palmer
First Assistant Director . . . Mike Topoozian
Second Assistant Director . . Stacey Beneville
Executive in Charge of Production
. . . . Erik Holmberg
Production Executive . . . . Dana Belcastro
Executive in Charge of Finance
. . . . Paul Prokop
Executive in Charge of Post Production
. . . . Jody Levin
Post Production Supervisor . . Frank Salvino

Special Consultant . . . . . Serena Rathbun
Production Liaison . . . . . . Glenn Mathias
Script Supervisor
. . . . Virginia Saenz McCarthy

Art Director . . . . John Kasarda
Assistant Art Director . . . . . Tom Warren
Art Department Coordinator . . Nora Kasarda
Art Department Production Assistant
. . . . Jennifer Santucci

Rendering Artists . . . . . Raymond Harvie
                            Grant Shaffer
                            David Duncan

Set Decorator . . . . . . Susan Bode-Tyson
Leadman . . . . Bruce Gross
On Set Dresser . . . . Jason Brown

Set Dressers
Catriona Crosby   D. Scott Gagnon
Patrick Woods   Hank Liebeskind

A Camera/Steadicam Operator
. . . . Michael Caracciolo
A Camera 1st Assistant . . . . Andy Voegeli
A Camera 2nd Assistant . . . . Adam Miller
B Camera Operator . . . . . . Dave Knox
B Camera 1st Assistant . . . . Larry Huston
B Camera 2nd Assistant
. . . . Mark Schwartzbard
Camera Loader . . . . Tim Ross

Process Effects . . . . . . William Hansard
Process Effects Coordinator . . Bill Hansard Jr.

Stills Photographer . . . Robert Zuckerman
Video Assist . . . . Brian Carmichael
Boom Operator . . . . Dave Pastecchi
Process Cameraman . . . . . Ray McMillan
Video Playback. . . . . Joe Tramell
Cableperson. . . . . Michelle Mader
Supervising Sound Editor. . . . . Will Riley
Re-recording Mixers
. . . . . Chris Jenkins & Chris Carpenter
Recordist . . . . Tim Webb
Production Accountant . . Richard Mancuso
First Assistant Accountant
. . . . Maryann Fondulas
Second Assistant Accountant . . . Steve Loff
Second Second Assistant Accountant
. . . . Catherine Generous
Accounting Assistant . . . . Michael Braun
Production Coordinator . . . . Greg Outcalt
Assistant Production Coordinator
. . . . Danielle Blumstein
Production Secretary . . . . Nicole Ferrari
Production Office Assistants . . Cristina Lois
Christine Putnam
Ganesh Hennings
Second Second Assistant Director
. . . . Gregory Palmer
Set Production Assistants . . . . Jason Booth
Fletcher Elkington
Kater Gordon
John Greenaway
Ryan Quinlan
Christina I. Rodriguez

Chief Lighting Technicians . . . Russ Engels
Tim Guinness
Best Boy Electrician . . . . Jon Leigh
Rigging Gaffer . . . . Doug Dalisera
Electricians. . . . . John Gilgar
Damian Gonzales
John Begley

Key Grip . . . . George Patsos
Best Boy Grip . . . . Gus Magalios
Dolly Grip . . . . Keith Bunting
Rigging Key Grip . . . . Billy Patsos
Grip . . . . Sonny Rea
Property Master. . . . . . . Martin Lasowitz
Scenic Artist . . . . Liz Bonaventura
Assistant Property Master . . Michael Jortner
Assistant Property. . . . . Tonero Williams
Standby Painter . . . . . . Stephen Shellooe
Greens. . . . . Amy Safhay
Special Effects Coordinator . . Michael Bird
First Assistant Film Editor . . . . . Ken Terry

Supervising Dialogue Editor . . Lisa Varetakis
Sound Effects Editor . . . . . D. Chris Smith
Dialogue Editors . . . . . Robert C. Jackson
Daniel S. Irwin MPSE
Assistant Sound Editor . . . . . Eryne Prine
Premixers . . . . Whitney Purple
Greg Townsend
Foley Walkers . . . . Alyson Moore
John Roesch
Foley Engineer. . . . . . . Mary Joe Long
Foley Editor. . . . . . Solange S. Schwabe
Foley Recordist . . . . Scott Morgan
ADR Voice Coordinator. . . . Leigh French
Department Head Makeup. . Linda Melazzo
Department Head Hair Stylist
. . . . Michelle Johnson
Makeup Artists . . . . Chip Williams
Randy Houston Mercer
Hair Stylist . . . . . Susie Mazzarese-Allison
Ms. Winslet's Wig by . . . . Renata
Ms. Connelly's Wig by . . . . Ira Senz
Assistant Costume Designer . . . Amy Roth
Costume Coordinator . . . Caroline Duncan
Costume Design for "Slutty Kay"
. . . . Melinda Eshelman
Set Costumers . . . . . Ghilaine Bouadana
Carmia Marshall
Background Costumer. . . . Natalie Arango
Ms. Winslet's Dresser . . . . Sandi Figueroa
Ms. Connelly's Dresser
. . . . Danielle Cadorette-Acehan
Costume Production Assistants
. . . . Alida P. Field
Raeanne Wright
Gabriella Kestler
Location Manager . . . . . . Mike Kriaris
Location P.A. . . . . Steven Carbajal
Assistant Location Managers . . . . Joe Guest
David McGuire
Location Assistants . . . . . Brian K. Barnes
Matt Kania
Parking Coordinator . . . . . Kerry Clark
Production Controller . . . . . Jon Davidson
Financial Advisor . . . . . Andrew Matthews
Production Resources . . . . Joshua Ravetch
Joe Steele
Supervising Production Coordinator
. . . . Emily Glatter
Business Affairs . . . . Erik Ellner
Production Attorney . . . Jeanette Hill-Yonis
Contract Administrator . . . Ginny Martino
Post Accountant. . . . . Judy Blinick
Additional Casting. . . . . . . Debra Zane
Tannis Vallely

Extras Casting. . . . . . . Sylvia Fay Casting
Extras Casting Coordinator . . . Lee Genick
Casting Assistants . . . . . Philip Huffman
           Laura Maxwell Scott
Assistant to Ms. Winslet . . Laurant Lambert
Assistant to Mr. Palmer . . Christine Marino
Assistant to Ms. Connelly . . Sasha Markova
Assistants to Mr. Berger & Mr. Yerxa
. . . . Jeremy Marks (New York)
       Cori Uchida (Los Angeles)
Visual Effects by . . . Big Film Design Corp
Visual Effects Supervisor. . Randall Balsmeyer
Digital Compositor . . . . Ella Boliver
Visual Effects Producer . . . . Tyra Hanshaw
Composite Artists . . . . . J. John Corbett
          Chris Halstead
Unit Publicist . . . . Weiman Seid
Set Medic . . . . Kristy Davenport
Ms. Winslet's Dialect Coach . . Susan Hegarty
Stand-in Ty Simpkins . . . . Vincent Sauli
Stand-in Sadie Goldstein . . . . . Elle Sauli
Stand-in Ms. Winslet . . . . Alyxx Morgen
Stand-in Ms. Connelly . . Carla Ochogrosso
Stand-in Mr. Wilson. . . . . Rick Johnson
Catering by . . . . Premiere Caterers
Craft Service by. . . . . David Dreishpoon
Craft Service Assistant . . . . . Diego Pina
Coffee kindly supplied by . . . Peet's Coffee
Transportation Captain. . . Steve Hammond
Transportation Co-Captain . . . Pete Clores
Second Unit Transportation Unit Captain
. . . . Billy McFadden
Ms Winslet's Driver . . . . . Herb Lieberz
Ms. Connelly's Driver . . . . Tom Aquino
Mr. Palmer's Driver . . . . . Tom Walsh
Mr. Berger's & Mr. Yerxa's Driver
. . . . John Moresco
Transportation Office Coordinator
. . . . Christina Schaich
Drivers . . . . . Ed Battista, Joe Blessington,
Juan Bryan, Paul Castiglione, Ron Cavazinni,
    Walter Chomow, Lew D'Angelo, Lance
    DeJesus, Frank Devine, Jerry Fetherstone,
Tim Garrett, Gary Gannetti, George Grenier,
    Joe Johnson, Jim Kelly, Jim Kober, Scott
    Lieberz, Rich Marino, Bill McFadden,
    Patrick McMahon, Joe Paustian, Thomas
    Planz, Frank Sanpietro, Mike Scalice,
    Joe Siringo, Joe Stapleton, Matt Stapleton,
    Drew Yanarella, Don Yeager

Second Unit
Director/Director of Photography
. . . . David Wagreich

First Assistant Director . . . Eric Henriquez
Second Assistant Directors . . Patrick Mangan
          Louis J. Guerra
A Camera Operator . . . . David Wagreich
A Camera First Assistant . . . Ronald Dennis
A Camera Second Assistant
. . . . Chris Raymond
B Camera Operator . . . . . Craig Cockerill
B Camera First Assistant . . . Fabio Iadeluca
B Camera Second Assistant
. . . . Branden Belmonte
Camera Loader . . . . Danny Feighdry
Sound Mixer . . . . Gary Alper
Boom Operator. . . . . Jerry Yuen
Gaffer . . . . Jon Leigh
Key Grip . . . . Billy Patsos
Executive in Charge of Music for New Line
. . . . Paul Broucek
Music Executive . . . . Erin Scully
Music Business Affairs Executives
. . . . Lori Silfen
          John F. X. Walsh
Music Contractor . . . . . . Leslie Morris
Music Preparation . . . . Julian Bratolyubov
Digital Audio . . . . Larry Mah

Music Conducted by . . . Thomas Newman
Orchestration. . . . . . . Thomas Pasatieri
Music Editor. . . . . Bill Bernstein
Assistant Music Editor . . . . Michael Zainer
Orchestra Recorded by . . . . Armin Steiner
Assistant Engineers . . . . . . Tim Lauber
          Greg Hayes
Music Scoring Mixer . . . . . Tommy Vicari

Music Recorded at
Signet Sound
The Newman Scoring Stage at
20th Century Fox
Paramount Scoring Stage
and
Capitol Records

Mixed at Signet Sound Services

Soundtrack Available from New Line
Records

"Fly Me To the Moon
(In Other Words)"
Written by Bart Howard
Conducted and Performed by
Sammy Nestico

"Battlefield Glory"
Written by Tom Hedden
Performed by Tom Hedden
Courtesy of NFL Films

"All In the Family"
Courtesy of Sony Pictures Television

Bloomberg Footage
Courtesy of Bloomberg Television

"The Charlie Rose Show" Courtesy of
Charlie Rose Productions

Fairfield Porter Artwork Courtesy of Hirschl
& Adler Gallery Private Collection

"Aftermath: Bosnia's Long Road to Peace"
Photographs by Sara Terry/Polaris
Published by Channel Photographics

"Children and Grief"
By J. William Worden
Published by
Guildford Publications, Inc.

"A Kiss For Little Bear"
Text © 1968 Else Homelund Minarik
Illustrations © 1968 Maurice Sendak
Used with permission of
HarperCollins Publishers

"Meet Mr. Product:
The Art of The Advertising Character"
By Masud Husain and Warren Dotz
Used with permission of
Chronicle Books LLC

"Bear and Kite"
By Cliff Wright
Used with permission of
Chronicle Books LLC

"The Runaway Bunny"
By Margaret Wise Brown
Text © 1970 Roberta Brown Rauch
Illustrations by
Edith T. Hurd, Clement Hurd, John
Thatcher Hurd and George Hellyer
Used with permission of
HarperCollins Publishers

Bozo Bop Bag Courtesy of
Larry Harmon Pictures

Clinical Consultants . . David Alexander MD
Herschel Knapp PhD
Marilyn Moore RN

Channel 5 News Segment
Segment Coordinators . . . . Leo Trombetta
Gina Caruso
Camera . . . . Molly Rokasy
Rights and Clearances by Entertainment
Clearances, Inc.
Cassandra Barbour and Laura Sevier

Risk Management
Laurie Cartwright and Juliana Selfridge

Production Safety by Jeff Egan

Insurance provided by
AON/Albert G. Ruben Insurance Services,
Inc.

Payroll by Cast and Crew Entertainment
Service, Inc.

Digital Intermediate by
EFilm

Digital Intermediate Colorist
. . . . Steven J. Scott
DI Editor . . . . Amy Pawlowski
DI Assistant Colorist . . . . . . Ntana Key
DI Project Manager. . . . . . Beth Dewey
Opticals by . . . . Pacific Title
Title Opticals by. . . . . Title House Digital
Negative Cutter. . . . . Rick Downey

Color Timer. . . . . . . Christopher Regan

Cameras Provided by
. . . . Camera Service Center
Cameras by . . . . ARRIFLEX
Lenses by. . . . . Zeiss & Angenieux
Hi-Speed Camera supplied by
. . . . Cine Magic International, Inc.

Transport Vehicles by . . . . . Haddads, Inc.

Originated on Kodak Motion Picture Film
Prints Released on Fujifilm
Colour by: DuArt
Prints by: Deluxe

ABOUT THE FILMMAKERS

TODD FIELD (Director, Producer, and Co-Writer)

Todd Field made his feature film debut at the Sundance Film Festival with *In the Bedroom*. Internationally acclaimed by critics, the film was named Best Picture of the Year by the *New York Times,* the *Wall Street Journal, New York Magazine, The New Yorker,* and the Los Angeles Film Critics Association. The film went on to receive five Academy Award® nominations, including Best Picture of the Year.

The New York Film Critics Circle, the Chicago Film Critics Association, and the Los Angeles Film Critics Association acknowledged Field for his work on the film, and the National Board of Review named him Director of the Year. Field received two Academy Award® nominations, a Golden Globe nomination, and an Independent Spirit Award. The British Film Institute recognized Field with the Satyajit Ray Award, and the American Film Institute honored him with the Franklin J. Schaffner Alumni Medal.

Field's short films include *Nonnie & Alex*, which premiered at the Sundance Film Festival and received a Special Jury Prize, and *When I Was a Boy,* which also premiered at the Sundance Film Festival and went on to the Film Society of Lincoln Center's New Directors/New Films Series at the Museum of Modern Art.

As an actor, Field has appeared in such films as Victor Nunez's *Ruby in Paradise* and Stanley Kubrick's *Eyes Wide Shut.*

TOM PERROTTA (Co-Writer)

Tom Perrotta is the author of five acclaimed works of fiction—*Little Children, Election* (made into the 1999 film, starring Reese Witherspoon and Matthew Broderick), *The Wishbones, Joe College,* and *Bad Haircut.* In addition to writing fiction and screenplays, he has also worked as a journalist and college teacher. His work has appeared in *GQ, Rolling Stone,* and *Best American Short Stories,* and has been translated into numerous languages. Tom lives with his family outside of Boston.

Little Children

NEW LINE CINEMA PRESENTS A BONA FIDE/STANDARD FILM COMPANY PRODUCTION KATE WINSLET JENNIFER CONNELLY "LITTLE CHILDREN" PATRICK WILSON JACKIE EARLE HALEY NOAH EMMERICH PHYLLIS SOMERVILLE CASTING BY TODD THALER MUSIC BY THOMAS NEWMAN COSTUME DESIGNER MELISSA ECONOMY DIRECTOR OF PHOTOGRAPHY ANTONIO CALVACHE ASSOCIATE PRODUCERS MICHELE WEISS LEON VITALI EDITOR LEO TROMBETTA, A.C.E. PRODUCTION DESIGNER DAVID GROPMAN EXECUTIVE PRODUCERS PATRICK PALMER TOBY EMMERICH KENT ALTERMAN PRODUCED BY ALBERT BERGER & RON YERXA AND TODD FIELD BASED ON THE NOVEL BY TOM PERROTTA SCREENPLAY BY TODD FIELD & TOM PERROTTA DIRECTED BY TODD FIELD